# HIS MAKER'S MARK

USA TODAY BEST SELLING AUTHOR
# KRISTEN PAINTER

*For Laura, without whom, I would have completely forgotten about this story. Thanks for being so pushy.*

**HIS MAKER'S MARK:**

A Standalone Paranormal Romance Novella

Copyright © 2024 Kristen Painter

All rights reserved. No part of this book may be reproduced in any form or by any electronic or mechanical means, including information storage and retrieval systems—except in the case of brief quotations embodied in critical articles or reviews—without permission in writing from the author.

This book is a work of fiction. The characters, events, and places portrayed in this book are products of the author's imagination and are either fictitious or are used fictitiously. Any similarity to real person, living or dead, is purely coincidental and not intended by the author.

Published in the United States of America

Annaleigh Bartow has one goal in mind. Save the last remaining examples of her grandfather's stonemasonry work. Unfortunately, that work is part of an old hotel scheduled for demolition.

And she's not the only one out to get a piece of it. When her attempt is thwarted by some ruthless thugs, an unexpected hero comes to her rescue. One who both frightens and fascinates her. One who will change her life in ways she can't imagine.

# CHAPTER ONE

A gust of wind lifted a few strands of Annaleigh Bartow's dark hair as she crouched against the exterior that housed the small lobby of the thirty-seventh floor's observation deck. For the first time in the many nights she'd been coming here, she was not alone.

Shuffled footsteps and shushed whispers had put her in this spot. Only a six-foot expanse of viewing platform separated her from a chest-high wall and a straight shot down to an empty stretch of Manhattan street. The section of building she leaned on rose up into another three stories. The door to the roof was on the opposite side. She'd never make it before she was discovered.

She glanced up. Could she climb to the next floor's windows? Most were broken or missing, but the ledges beneath them, supported with acanthus leaf corbels, were wide and sturdy.

This part of the old hotel was the most decorated, and the reason she'd risked coming back was here. Despite her best efforts to save it, this building was coming down. Didn't matter to the city fathers that those carvings were some of the last remaining work her grandfather, Henry William Bartow, had done. All they cared about was progress. And the tax dollars a new condo building would bring. The only memories she'd have of that fantastic stonework would be the pictures she took.

Muted laughter brought her head back down. Whoever had followed her here had probably seen her sneaking into the abandoned building with her camera equipment and figured she'd be an easy target.

Her searching hand closed around a rusted length of pipe. A target, yes. Easy, no. She listened, trying to quiet the blood rushing through her veins. Beeping horns and wailing sirens drifted up from the street, but at this height, they were merely background to the wind whistling past the building's sharp lines and carved edges.

If only there were a moon, but the night was as dark as the city sky could be, a hazing, sooty gray. No stars, no moon, no light. And at this height, the faint glow from the streets didn't reach very far.

The crunch of a footfall came from the left. Another followed it. Her heart jumped into overdrive, and an idea formed in her adrenalin-flushed brain. As quietly as she could, she rested the pipe at her feet and opened her camera bag. Slowly, she eased out the old Nikon, thankful the flash was still attached, then positioned the bag and the camera in the direction of the noise. She grabbed the flash remote, punched in the desired sequence, stuck it in her pocket, then gripped the pipe and pushed to her feet.

Worst case scenario, the police would have pictures of her attackers. If they recovered the camera. Or found her body before the building was demolished. She rolled her eyes at her lack of positive thinking, but then, the city hadn't given her much to be positive about lately.

The footsteps came closer.

*Breathe. Wait. Relax.* A muscle in her jaw twitched. So much for relaxing. She closed her eyes. Pushed the remote button. It was followed by a soft click then the lightning quick burst filtered through her lids. Wind swept away the surprised curses of her would-be attackers. She dropped the remote and launched herself around the corner, swinging her makeshift weapon with two hands and a guttural roar.

Three man-sized shapes stumbled in the darkness, seemingly disoriented from the flash. One ran for the exit immediately, leaving the other two behind. She went for the head of the one wielding a knife. Metal connected with bone. The impact jarred her arms. She staggered back.

The man she'd hit collapsed, dropping his blade. The other lunged for her, catching the end of the pipe as she tried to retreat. He ripped it out of her hand. The pipe's jagged edge tore across her palm in a searing line of pain before clattering to the ground behind him. She squeezed her fist, warm liquid oozing between her fingers. A sharp wash of queasiness spun through her. She forced it away too late.

The man grabbed her, yanked her close. He stank of booze and cigarettes and the sour stench earned through a complete disregard for personal hygiene. "We were just gonna take your stuff, but now I think we'll have a little more fun."

Another soft click. She squeezed her lids down. Another flash. She opened her eyes. Her attacker looked dazed.

"Let's start with this." She stomped his instep, shoved him away, and raced for the wall. Hopefully, the blinding flash would buy her a few seconds. Thank God she'd worn sneakers. Her foot found purchase in the notched marble, and she pushed up, reaching for one of the medallions dividing the 57th floor windows.

She grabbed hold and pulled, getting high enough to latch onto the clawed foot of the main reason she'd come tonight, the building's last intact gargoyle. Her hand, slick with blood, slipped off the winged creature until only her fingertips curled over the beast's thick limestone toes.

"Help me," she whispered. His leonine face stared passively into the city, his visage as still as the stone he'd had been carved from.

A hand closed around her ankle and yanked. She came tumbling down, landing hard on her back. The air left her body in a hard gasp. Another click. Another flash.

The man grabbed a handful of her leather jacket and

jerked her to her feet. "You're making me work, and I don't like to work."

"By the smell of you, you don't like to shower either."

Cursing, he backhanded her, his enormous hand making contact with her jaw and cheek. "You don't know when to shut up, do you girlie?"

Her eyes watered, the taste of copper filled her mouth, and fear chilled her skin. She spat the blood out. Her head was spinning. He'd clocked her pretty hard. This wasn't going the way she'd hoped. "Let go of me."

"Sure, princess. When I'm done with you." He shook her, hard, then started unbuckling his belt.

His partner on the ground moaned and crawled for his knife. "Hit her again, she busted my head open."

"Might as well. I don't care if she's conscious or not." With a laugh, her captor balled his fist and connected with her temple. The skyline tilted, and she went down. The marble tiles were cold and gritty beneath her cheek. Something dark swept across the charcoal sky.

Another click. Another flash. Then everything went black.

# CHAPTER TWO

Blood. Warm and familiar, but also female.

*Female.*

For the first time in nearly eighty years, Vasmir recognized the beckoning of a human. She who called him stood below, with two others. There had been a third man, but he had bolted at the flash of light. Vasmir inhaled, drawing her tantalizing fragrance into his nostrils. Her blood. Her command.

But also the stench of the men below. He had smelled them before. Thieves. Destroyers. The lowest of their kind.

He ignored them because he realized he knew her. Recognized her. Many, many years ago, he'd seen her with his maker. She'd been a small child then. The men he didn't know. Perhaps they were—

The upright human male struck her, knocked her down. A burst of light illuminated the scene, outlining the intent on the man's face.

Red edged Vasmir's sight and life coursed into his cold heart like a blast of fire, dispelling the chill of his stone shell and giving him purpose. He was born to this. To protect. To dispel evil. He could do nothing less.

With the bone-jarring crack of stone breaking away from stone, he spread his wings, and leapt into the night air to answer her call. Instantly, his full size came upon him, stretching his chiseled body and elongating his muscles.

At the sudden noise, the men looked up. Disbelief, then terror filled their faces, drawing them into masks as grotesque as the carvings he'd once called brothers. Another brilliant flash of light outlined them like rabbits in a field. Swooping down, he clamped his great, sickle-tipped fingers around their throats and rose again, his prey dangling, gasping, goggle-eyed and limp. He took off toward the river, keeping his pace slow until his body adjusted to the rapid change her blood had thrust upon it.

"You...you aren't real," the one who'd hit her croaked. He pried at Vasmir's fingers. The stench of excrement wafted from the other and a large stain soiled the man's already filthy pants. He did not seem to be awake.

Vasmir bent his head to look into their eyes. Already his wings softened in the cool night air, quieting as he flew. "Do you not see me? Are you not clutched in my grasp?"

The man's mouth gaped, but no sound emerged. Jagged red lines striated the whites of his eyes. He glanced down at the city.

Vasmir peered closer. "Why did you hurt her?"

The man struggled to speak. Vasmir relaxed his hand and the man's eyes went even wider. He clung to Vasmir's wrist. "Don't drop me, please don't drop me. I won't hurt anyone ever again, I swear."

Not an answer. Vasmir tightened his grip. "Why did you hurt her?"

The man tried to shake his head. "We..." he wheezed. "Just wanted to have some fun—"

"Fun?" Anger grew in Vasmir's belly. He had spent many years watching humans. He understood much about them and their strange ways, but hitting someone and causing them to bleed was not having fun. Not for the one who bled. "You hurt her who called me. For that, you must be dealt with. Who sent you to the building?"

"No one," the man answered a little too quickly.

"Liar," Vasmir snarled. "Who sent you? Tell me the truth and I might spare you."

The man seemed to consider that. "Whatever you're gonna do to me won't be as bad as what he'd do. I ain't telling you."

Vasmir sensed the man meant that. Which meant he was done with both of them.

A slight change in the plane of his body and he plunged lower, causing the lucid man to shriek and Soiled Pants to lift his drooping head.

"What...where are we?" Soiled Pants blinked hard. A bloody bruise, dark and sticky like a crushed rose, adorned his temple. The thought that she who called him had placed it there soothed Vasmir. Perhaps he would not kill these men after all. Then again what was to stop them from attacking another woman and making her their victim?

Soiled Pants stared at Vasmir. One hand reached out as if to touch Vasmir's body to determine whether or not what he saw was real.

Vasmir bared his teeth in a seldom-used grin. "Do not touch me, human."

Soiled Pants' hand dropped, his eyes rolled back in his head, and he faded away once again.

The river swelled below, dark and oily. Streaks of yellow reflected light rippled over the water. Vasmir dipped until the surface shimmered inches from the feet of the attackers. They had hurt her. Planned to hurt her further. Their lives were of no concern to him. To protect. To dispel evil. Those things mattered. He could nothing less for her who had called him. And she still lay upon the roof. Hurt. Alone. In need of him.

Straightening his wings, he relaxed his grip and let them drop.

Their cries faded as he wheeled mid-air and flew for home. Completely warmed up, he covered the distance back to the building in half the time. He landed out of sight, in case she'd woken while he was gone. He knew too well how most humans reacted to his kind. His brothers had paid the price for it. He would not follow them, not now that he'd been given purpose.

Easing around the rooftop deck, he craned to see her. She lay where he'd left her. Not good. Doing his best to keep his clawed toes from digging up the marble, he picked his way to her.

Blood trickled from the corner of her mouth. He licked his thumb, then wiped it away. She was cold. Too cold. He pressed the back of his hand to her pale throat. Her skin warmed beneath his touch. A strong pulse beat out a rhythm. That was good. She had to survive. Then he noticed one of her eyes already swelled with a bruise.

An ancient curse in a language unspeakable by human tongues spun from his lips. He lifted his head skyward and willed the anger away. The men had been dealt with. Now he must do what he could to care for her.

She needed to be inside. He would have to carry her. He flexed his hands, staring at his claws. He would hurt her with those. He could not allow that to happen. Glancing around, he found a length of metal pipe nearby. He snatched it up and vaulted skyward, flying to the top of the building and landing there.

Kneeling, he rested one hand on the ground and took up the pipe in the other. Gritting his teeth, he brought the pipe down hard across his thumb claw. The pain nearly doubled him. Saliva pooled in his mouth with the nauseous rise of his belly. For the one who called him, he could do this.

Nine times more he cracked the pipe against his offending talons, breaking them from his body and making himself safe for her. At last, he rose, body trembling with the echoes of pain, and flew back to her side.

He bent and lifted her into his embrace. A bright flash of light illuminated the scene, then all went dark again. He looked in the direction of the light. There on the ground was the device she'd been using the last few nights. Always pointing it at him and the building. Clutching it like it mattered to her a great deal. He would take care of that later. Right now, she was most important.

Her dark hair spilled over his arm, her pale skin like smooth silk compared to the rough gravel of his. She was neither too heavy nor too light, her body a softly curving wonder that left him in awe. Never had one such as he held one such as her.

The pain in his hands forgotten, he carried her into the building.

# CHAPTER THREE

Shafts of sun pierced the dirty windows, compounding the throbbing in Annaleigh's head. Where was she and why did she feel like she'd been run through a super-sized pasta machine? Stone tiles made an uncomfortable bed. Judging by the angle of the light coming into the room, the day would soon be drawing to a close.

Thankfully, today was Sunday and the shop was closed so she wouldn't get into trouble for missing work.

Less optimal was the fact that she had no idea where she was.

She pushed to her elbows and blinked at the grit in her eyes. Pain danced across her skull and into her jaw, bringing with it a rush of memory. Last night had not been a good one. She went to clutch her head and new pain torched her hand. A blood-crusted cut traversed her palm. The pipe. Great, she was probably going to need a tetanus shot for that.

What else was she going to need? She tentatively pressed her fingers over her face and found several tender spots. One of her eyes was a little swollen.

Grimacing, she examined the rest of her body, praying not to find what she most suspected...

But no. The rest of her felt okay. Her back was sore from where she'd fallen, but there was no pain in the most intimate parts of her body. She'd not been assaulted further.

How had she not been assaulted? Isn't that what those two awful men had intended? And how had she ended up inside the hotel? Had they dragged her in here? She didn't think so.

If they had, they would had done more to her. Had their fun. But there was no sign of that. Her clothing was all intact.

She must have dragged herself in here. But that didn't seem right. All she remembered was the man hitting her, then she'd fallen as everything went black. Then nothing. Dragging herself in here would've been impossible, wouldn't it?

Maybe she'd woken up, gotten inside, then blacked out again? There was no other explanation that she could think of.

She sighed and her stomach growled, a good motivator to get up and moving. She carefully twisted to her side, knocking over a bottle of water in the process.

A second bottle stood beside it and next to that, two long foil-wrapped packages that looked remarkably like street vendor hotdogs. Her camera, camera case, and tripod were there, too.

Okay, she might have dragged herself in here, but she

definitely had not gone out and gotten food from the Weiner King cart on the corner. It was also highly unlikely she would have remembered her camera equipment, but if she had, she would have tucked the Nikon back into the bag.

Someone else had been here.

She grabbed a bottle of water, checked that the seal was in place, then cracked it open and sucked half of it down. The water tasted better than any she'd had in a long time. She drank a little more, contemplating the hotdogs. Probably not a good idea, regardless of the growling in her stomach. She sighed and took inventory of the lobby. She'd been in here before and it looked pretty much the same. Yellowed papers blown into the corners, random discarded clothing, fast food wrappers, the lingering stench of body odor and urine, and an old club chair with the stuffing ripped out. Yep, all the usual stuff.

Except for the gouges in the once beautiful granite flooring.

Five evenly spaced furrows set at alternating interludes marked a path to her, then back to the door. She shivered at the thought of what could do that. Because it had to be a what, didn't it? No person she knew left those kinds of tracks.

Forget the hotdogs and her aches and pains, she had to get out of here. She grabbed her camera and started to tuck it into the bag, then stopped cold. Hadn't she set the remote to shoot pics during the whole ordeal?

Hands shaking, she powered up the Nikon, grateful it had shut itself down and preserved some battery power, and paged through the pictures of the building and its carvings until she came to one that made the breath catch in her chest.

The two men from last night creeping in her direction. In the harsh light of the flash, they looked as disgusting as she remembered them.

The next shot showed the man she'd hit on the ground, the other one holding her as she struggled to get away. Hot angry tears blurred her vision. She scrubbed the back of her hand across her eyes, but quickly pulled it away as she touched a painful spot. She carefully felt the area. Her one eye was swollen from where the man had hit her. A feeling of helplessness coursed through her as she relived the moment.

The next had her on her back, him standing over her. She bit her lip. In that moment, on that cold tiled roof, she'd known exactly what he'd intended to do to her, but somehow it hadn't happened. She had no memory beyond this moment.

Swallowing, she clicked the button and advanced to the next picture. Her on the ground, the two men looking skyward with absolute terror contorting their faces. What had they seen?

The next three pictures were of her, alone on the rooftop. The men were gone. How could they vanish like that? Had they jumped? Unlikely. Run off that quickly? Also pretty unlikely.

She clicked the button, expecting more of the same. Instead, she stared harder at the small screen, trying to understand what she was seeing. She recognized herself lying there, but that's where reality seemed to break. She shook her head. It couldn't be. Could it? This was photographic evidence after all.

Those stories her father had told her, stories his grandfather had told him. They were just fairytales. Wild yarns. This...this thing, this creature bending over her couldn't be real.

Her gaze traveled to the gouges on the floor, then back to the picture for a long moment. Finally, she lifted her head and stared out to the deck where everything had taken place.

There was only one way to find out.

Camera in hand, she picked her way past the refuse and the slashes notched into the flooring and walked out onto the deck. Slowly, she grabbed hold of her frayed nerves and approached the creature. In the waning light of day, he seemed less ferocious than he did at night. His muscled body more at rest than crouched to pounce.

Even his claws—wait, now. She took another step closer. The claws on his hands were gone. Broken off, it looked like. He'd been whole last night, she was sure of it. Lifting her camera, she flipped back past the pictures of the incident to the ones she taken with her tripod and flash. Yes. Whole. Whatever had happened to him had happened last night. There was no other explanation.

The claws on his feet were fine. Blood stained the one

closest to her. Her blood, from when she'd touched him as she'd tried to climb up and away. She felt sick suddenly. Bile rose in her throat, and she forced it down, noticing that his unbroken claws also looked about the right size and separation to have made the grooves in the lobby floor.

Disbelief made her head dizzy and her mouth dry. If there had been chair, she would have sat in it. Instead, she pressed forward until she stood directly below him. It. Whatever the creature was.

Feeling one hundred percent the fool, she stuck the camera into the air, viewing screen faced at him. "I have your picture."

Nothing. No movement. No blink of an eye. He just stared down into the city.

She thrust the camera higher. "I have your picture. I know you're real." That was a lie. She knew nothing anymore. Maybe the knock to her head had damaged more than just her face. Maybe her brain was broken. Maybe she *had* been assaulted and beaten and was actually lying in a hospital bed somewhere in a coma.

The sun slipped lower, throwing the roof into shadow.

"I know you're real," she whispered, lowering the camera. She *wanted* to believe what her camera showed her. The alternative held no appeal. "If you are, I won't tell anyone," she added.

Nothing.

A few more minutes and it would be dark, and she

still had to get out of this building *and* this neighborhood intact. With forced effort, she went back inside, packed up her camera, collapsed her tripod and headed for the stairs, the second bottle of water in her hand. Two steps down, she stopped and looked back.

She really ought to get a shot of the broken claws and the grooved flooring. Just to prove to herself she wasn't crazy.

She snapped a few shots in the lobby, then went back out to the deck. Crap. She would be walking home in the dark after all. Two quick pictures and she tucked the camera away, then sighed as she stared at him one last time.

The building was coming down soon. And then he'd be no more. The thought pained her more than her bruises.

"I don't know if you're real or not, but I think you saved my life last night. You must have also gotten me that water and the food. Thank you."

With that she turned and trudged back toward the lobby. A strange cracking sound froze her solid in her tracks.

"You are welcome."

# CHAPTER FOUR

She who called him went still as the stone he was carved from. Had some strange shift of magic caused her to become fixed when he came to life? She had not moved last night after he had come to life, either, but he'd assumed that was because she had been struck.

He reached for her, his broken fingers brushing the ends of her brown locks.

She turned, and he snapped his hand back. For a moment, she just stared, so he stared back. Paler than he remembered, jaw bruised, eye purpling, she was no less beautiful than the first time she'd come to flash her light at him.

"What did you say?" The breathy tone of her voice made her sound like she'd been running, but her open mouth and raised brow showed her fear.

He bent his head to lower himself to her eye level. She had no reason to fear him. "I said you are welcome."

"You're a statue." She shook her head, her shoulders raising in a dismissive shrug. "You're not real." She waved her hand like brushing flies away. "You're, you're...you're a—"

"A beast," he finished for her, dropping his head. How could she think otherwise? He knew what she saw, the uncomfortable size of him, the feline-cast of his face, the excess of muscle he'd been carved with.

"No," she said softly. "I was going to say gargoyle."

That brought his head back up. "Yes, I am. And yes, I am a statue, and no, I'm not real. Not by the standards of your world. But in mine, I am very real. My flesh and blood are not your flesh and blood, but here I stand before you. Alive. Because of you."

Her shapely brows went a touch higher. "What do you mean because of me?"

"You called me."

"I called you." She glanced back toward the ledge he spent his days crouched upon. "You mean when I was trying to get away from those guys?"

He nodded. "Your blood and your desire for my help. With those things, you brought me into your world."

"But you said yourself you're not real."

Capturing her soft hand, he placed it against the hard wall of his chest. "Do I feel real?" She certainly did. Life and heat and sweetness pulsed against his palm, the delicate bones of her hand reminded him of the small birds that sometimes sought him out as shelter.

Her fingers pressed against him, her chest rising and falling with the beat of one breath before she answered.

"Yes. And no." She swallowed but didn't remove her hand. "I don't understand this."

"Must you understand this magic to accept me?" This close, the stormy green of her eyes amazed him. She who called him was the most beautiful of humans. He was, as were all his called brethren, desperate to please the one who'd called him.

Her hand relaxed. "Did you save me from those men?"

"Yes. I did as you commanded. I helped. They won't hurt you again."

She slowly pulled her hand away. Her eyes hardened in a way that caused an emptiness inside him. "Did you… toss them off the building?"

The emptiness vanished and he started to smile, then caught himself lest he frighten her again. "No."

"Are they dead?"

"Can humans swim?"

"Most of them, yes. Why?"

His turn to shrug. "They are probably not dead then. I cannot say for sure."

She opened her mouth, then pursed her lips. "Maybe it's better I don't know."

He just nodded. "It is."

"Do you have a name?"

"Vasmir."

She held her hand out. "I'm Annaleigh."

"Annaleigh." Since the first day he'd seen her in the company of his maker so many years ago, he'd wondered about her name. To speak it now seemed a gift. He said it again. "Annaleigh."

"You're supposed to shake my hand." The faintest hint of a smile played at the corner of her rose-hued mouth even as apprehension filled her gaze.

He nodded. "Yes, I've seen humans do this." He reached out and carefully clasped her hand. She might be somewhat afraid of him, but not so much that she wouldn't touch him. She'd actually asked for him to do so. The warmth his heart had absorbed from the sun suffused through him. Was this what happiness felt like to humans? If so, he would find a way to make her happy. Learn what it took to keep her happy.

Her grip tightened and she turned his hand so that his fingers were visible to her. She seemed to be studying what she saw, and he was content to let her. He was hers to command, whether she knew it or not.

"What happened to your claws? You had them last night. Before everything happened." She stared up from beneath soot-dark lashes, her eyes glimmering in the fading twilight. A strong breeze whipped past.

"I..." He did not know what to tell her. The truth? And have her know she'd been the cause of his pain, even though he would willingly bear it a thousand times over? And yet, what choice did he have? He was powerless to tell her falsehoods. The called might never lie to those who called them. It was the way of things.

Her hand grew hot on his. "It was those men, wasn't

it? They did this to you." Anger flashed in her green eyes. Anger at a perceived wrong that he'd been the recipient of. The very thought that he could cause such emotion in her dizzied his head like diving too fast through an open sky.

"No." How easy it would be to let that thieving duo take the blame. To bask in the warmth of her righteous anger. He pulled his hand away. "I did this to myself."

Her brows drew together as she made a face, her eyes holding questions. "What? Why would you do such a thing?"

He lifted both hands, palms up, and curled his fingers in. "I did not want to injure you any more than you already had been."

Her mouth gaped and the sudden flash of realization blanked all other expression from her face, save one of utter sadness. "Oh, Vasmir."

His name on her lips. Joy spiraled through him, a desperate freefall of sensation that made him long for more. "I would do it again. Gladly."

She grabbed his hands and drew them against her cheeks. "You saved my life." She brought his fingers to her mouth and kissed the broken tips. "How can I ever repay you?"

For a moment, he couldn't answer. The swell of pleasure inside him was so great it choked the words from his throat, made his vision blur at the edges. He wanted to preen like a cat in the sun. "There is no payment to be made. You've given me life."

Squeezing his hands, she smiled. "So you're free of this building then?"

He tipped his head. "No, this is my home. I must always return here when the sun rises. But when it sets, I am yours."

"Oh no, no, that can't be. You don't need this building to live, you can't." The smile was gone, twisted into a grimace of panic and desperation.

"Yes, I am sorry, but I must return here. It's my home." He had not meant to upset her, but she must understand. "Surely, you have a home you must return to as well."

She nodded, slow and sad. "Yes, but my home isn't going to be destroyed in two days."

# CHAPTER FIVE

Vasmir's hands had been sun-warmed, but at Annaleigh's words they went icy cold in her grasp, his eyes glittering dark as he spoke. "What do you mean destroyed?"

"The city is tearing this building down." Bitter tears burned her lids. The thought of Vasmir being destroyed along with the rest of the building stabbed daggers into her heart. This amazing creature, this incredible being, this...this *man*, gone. "Didn't you see the chain link fence they've put up around the property? They've already begun running the lines for the explosives."

"I saw that, but I did not understand it."

She scrubbed a hand over her face, wincing at the bruises she'd forgotten. "I've tried to stop them, tried to show them with my pictures what incredible artistry they'll be demolishing. Tried to tell them the last remaining work of my grandfather will be destroyed along with the building, but they don't care."

"This is my home." He straightened to his full, impressive height. "Without this building I cannot exist. I am a part of it."

"What about those men? They were going to pry you off the building and take you. Couldn't I do the same thing somehow? Get you off the building?" Keep you alive, she wanted to add, but the words hurt too much just thinking them.

"Those men destroyed my brothers with their careless greed. Taking me from this building is not an easy thing."

*Think, think.* She swallowed down a swell of rising panic. "There are salvage companies. I could call one, see what they would charge. Or maybe I could petition the historical society again." Not that she had a lot of money or influence. But for him, she would find a way. "I'll save you. I promise."

He shook his head, eyes downcast. "Do not promise. I would not have you bear the guilt of breaking your word. I will accept my fate if only..."

"What? Anything. Just tell me."

He turned slightly, the orange glow of the setting sun outlining his great profile. "It is, perhaps, too bold a thing to ask."

*Bold?* She grabbed his arm, her hand barely spanning the width of his rock hard forearm. "You saved my life. You have the right to ask me anything."

Closing his eyes, he swallowed, then reopened them, staring hard at her hand.

He must not like to be touched. She started to move it.

"Don't take your hand away. I like that you are not afraid to touch me."

She kept her hand where it was. "Then tell me what it is you need." Her voice had thinned to a whisper, but that didn't disguise the need threading her veins. He would be gone in two days. The time for ignoring her feelings and being coy was long past.

His face lifted enough to find her eyes. "I would walk beside you. Be with you. Not as I am, but as I could be, if you wish it."

"What do you mean, if I wish it?"

"I can take human form, if you but grant me one thing. A single boon." His gaze shifted for a moment to her lips.

"You can? Of course, anything. What do I have to do to grant this boon?" Not that she was exactly sure what a boon was anyway.

"You would have to…" He shook his head. "It's too much to ask."

"Just tell me."

He exhaled and stared out at the city. "To begin with, you would have to kiss me. And I cannot ask that. Not after what happened to you this night."

He was right. The memories of that man's hands on her, of him unbuckling his belt, of his intentions, they were still fresh.

Kissing anyone, even Vasmir, felt like something she needed to think about. "I don't know if I—"

"There is nothing for you to do, because I am not asking. It is too great a boon."

"I don't know about that, but I would like a day to think about it. I know time is short, but one day won't make much difference."

"No. One day will not."

She stared at him, studying his face. She had pictures of him, but those wouldn't compare to seeing him in person. "I'll be back tomorrow. At dusk. I promise."

"I know you will. You have come every night."

Trying to save this place, but now all that mattered was saving him. "Have a good night."

"How will you get home safely?"

"You think those men—"

"No, not them. But this area. I see from my perch the things that happen on the streets. It is not safe for a woman alone."

He was right about that. She'd been lucky so far. But after what had happened here yesterday evening, she'd begun to think her luck had run out. "Maybe you could follow me? Overhead, I mean?"

"Yes. I will do that. And if anyone should try to harm you, I will be sure they do not."

She smiled. "Thank you, Vasmir."

He bowed. "I am at your service, Annaleigh." Then he jumped and shot straight into the sky, his wings expanding to catch the wind.

Her own gargoyle bodyguard. She took one last look then headed down to the street. It was a long way without a working elevator, but when she emerged from the building, he was there, overhead, waiting. Just a darker shape against the night sky and if she hadn't known what to look for, she never would have seen him.

She squeezed through a gap in the chain-link fence and made her way home. At her building, she took another look skyward. She scanned in both directions but didn't see him. He must have already gone back to the hotel.

She went inside, climbed the three flights of stairs to her tiny studio apartment and quickly got ready for bed. Getting into bed meant climbing the narrow set of ladder-like steps that led up to the sleeping loft. The steps probably weren't to code, but she'd be the last one to complain.

This tiny studio, which was barely big enough to turn around in, was all she could afford. Outside of the small bathroom, the space was all one room. The kitchen, if it could be called that, was two burners and a mini-fridge. But at least it was her space.

She only had it because she'd known the person who'd lived here previously, and they'd worked out a deal for her to take over the lease. From the loft, which held a mattress, box springs, and a wooden crate she'd painted white to serve as a nightstand, she could see out the windows, the best feature of the studio.

Her eyes searched the slice of visible sky. Was he out there? Soaring through the darkness? Thinking about her?

As she lay in bed, she looked through the photos on her camera again. Kissing Vasmir wasn't that big of a deal. Not if it meant saving him. She'd do anything to save him. Especially now that she knew he'd saved her.

She'd tell him tomorrow. She'd go to the hotel right after work. She put her camera down and sighed. Another day at Tidwell's Antiques, another day dealing with clients who had more money than they knew what to do with.

Must be nice, she thought. She drifted off, dreaming of what it would be like to buy the old hotel and bring it back to life.

With Vasmir at her side.

# CHAPTER SIX

He perched on the ledge of the building across from the one she'd gone into. Somewhere, safe inside of that very plain steel and concrete tower, was she who had called him. She deserved better than such a place to call home, but he was glad she'd returned there without incident.

He wondered if the man who'd hired the two thieves was waiting for his friends. What would he do if they never returned? Would he take it out on Annaleigh?

Vasmir had no way of knowing if that man knew her address. No one had followed her home, that much he'd made sure of. He had worried that man might accost Annaleigh. No, worried was not right. He had *anticipated* it. Hoped for it, in a small way.

He would not have wanted her to be scared again, but dealing with that man, eliminating him, as Vasmir had the others, would have been good. He would have dealt with the man before he had a chance to frighten Annaleigh.

Wind whistled past. The urge to fly was strong, but the hopes that he might see Annaleigh one more time was stronger. Which of those windows was she behind? Very few had lights on, making it impossible to tell.

Would he see her again? Or had telling her about the kiss been too much? He had reason to believe it might have been. He never should have mentioned it. Not after what she'd been through already.

But she had said she would be back and he had no reason not to believe her. She would not have lied to him. He could not fathom that. She was the ancestor of his maker, a true and honest man as ever there had been.

Vasmir had been created by him and was just as true and honest. That was the way of things.

As for Annaleigh, he would just have to wait. And hope.

He watched the building a little while longer, peering into the windows, but Annaleigh was nowhere to be seen. He leaped off the ledge and stretched his wings, taking flight. He climbed higher so that he could not be seen, although few citizens of the city looked up.

He coasted on the drafts for a while, letting the wind take him where it might as his mind did the same. Annaleigh permeated his thoughts. He had not been able to tell her what else would be required of her besides the kiss.

He wasn't sure the rest of it would matter.

After a while, he gave a mighty shove with his wings and changed direction. He went out over the river. He looked for any sign of the men, but as he had suspected, there was nothing. No sign of them. No sign they had been found.

He went back to the hotel, swooping around it to see the three other corners that had once been home to his brethren. Nothing remained of them but blank spaces. Except in the case of Detre, where there was still one hand and wrist, and one leg up to the knee.

The rest of him had plummeted to the earth when the two thieves had tried to pry him loose. The shattered pieces were now lost amongst the debris field created by the men who had been working at the hotel. Preparing it, he now knew, for demolition.

It would have been better if his brothers could have been saved, but then again, maybe their outcome was as it was meant to be. At least they would not have to witness what he would. The destruction of their home. And perhaps his own destruction.

He settled onto his perch, his head tilted so he could see the city below. Annaleigh would not abandon him, would she? He prayed not.

But if she did...he was grateful to have met her all the same. Grateful that for one brief span of time, he had been useful to her. He hoped his maker would be proud.

Muted pink light edged the horizon. Dawn was coming. With the sun's rise, he would turn to stone again.

Then all he would be able to do was wait.

Annaleigh leaned against one of the counters and yawned. These late nights at the old hotel were ruining her sleep.

Mr. Tidwell cleared his throat sharply. "Is work keeping you from something?"

She straightened. "No, sorry, sir. Late night is all." He'd already questioned her about why her makeup was so heavy today. She'd explained she'd tripped and given herself a black eye and had done her best to conceal it, but his expression said he hadn't totally believed that.

He could believe what he wanted. Black eyes weren't a crime.

Now he gave her a cutting look, but she was spared further conversation by a customer coming in. He flashed his fake smile at the woman. "Mrs. Crofton, how nice to see you. Dare I hope this is about the jewelry we discussed last week?"

"It might be," Mrs. Crofton replied.

Annaleigh busied herself in the fine arts section with a feather duster. She was tired, but her energy would come back as soon as she was free of this place and able to see Vasmir again. She smiled as she worked.

She was going to kiss him tonight. She was going to kiss him and save him. She supposed she shouldn't think of it in such romantic terms, but it all seemed very much like a fairy tale come to life to her.

A gargoyle that could become human if only she kissed him. Who wouldn't think that was like something out of a storybook?

"Annaleigh?" Mr. Tidwell called out for her. "Get Mrs. Crofton a cup of Darjeeling, would you? I'll take a cup, too. We'll be in my office."

"Yes, sir." Annaleigh put the feather duster away and went to make tea. She knew Mr. Tidwell would expect a little plate of shortbread cookies, too. He always did, even if he acted like it was such a surprise when she brought them in.

She made the tea, fixed a plate of cookies, then carried it all in on the silver tray Mr. Tidwell liked the employees to use. She knocked on his office door, waited until he acknowledged her, then went in.

Mr. Tidwell smiled brightly. "You brought shortbread! What a nice surprise."

"Oh," Mrs. Crofton said. "I do love shortbread."

Mrs. Crofton had an array of jewelry pieces set out on Mr. Tidwell's desk. He'd placed a velvet tray on it for that purpose. A string of fat creamy white South Sea pearls with a diamond clasp, an art deco diamond and emerald bracelet, a diamond circle pin, a ruby and diamond ring with a matching pair of dangling earrings, and a lady's diamond watch.

The money earned from the sale of one of those items alone would change Annaleigh's life. It was hard to struggle all the time. The worrying got so old. So tiring.

She only had her camera because it had once belonged to her father.

She served the tea and cookies with a smile that hid

her thoughts. Someday, things would get easier. They had to.

Could helping Vasmir be a part of the change she so desperately needed?

She left the office while pondering that idea, but that just brought new questions to mind. Once he was no longer attached to the hotel, where would he live? He'd be human then. Basically. Wouldn't he?

Was he planning on staying with her? It wasn't the worst solution, but her apartment was so tiny that having a creature Vasmir's size in it would probably fill it completely. But if he could work and help with bills, that would actually be helpful.

But what kind of work could a former gargoyle do? He was big enough to be a bouncer. But he wouldn't have any kind of ID. Were there clubs willing to hire someone who was undocumented?

She sighed as she put the tray away in the makeshift kitchen area. She couldn't wait to see him again. She had a lot of questions that needed to be answered.

# CHAPTER SEVEN

Frozen inside his stone form, Vasmir watched the world pass by beneath him. If Annaleigh was coming tonight, she would come soon. The sun was sinking toward the horizon. He would be free to move soon.

Down below him, within the confines of the fence the construction men had set up, things had gotten busier. All day men had traveled around the site. Carrying things, moving things, pointing, rearranging, taking things out, taking things in.

The level of activity had confused him. What was going on down there? Was it all in preparation to demolish his home?

Home. The only home he'd ever known. But he couldn't think of this place that way any longer. Although if Annaleigh didn't show up, it would be more than just his home. It would be his tomb. He would be destroyed right along with the building.

Even if she didn't come tonight, he would fly. He would fly as much as he could in the time he had left. He would not waste the remaining hours of his existence by doing nothing.

There was new movement below. Someone at the fence. He tracked them, an easy feat even in the dimness of dusk. If he'd been able to smile, he would have.

Annaleigh had arrived.

The hotel looked very different than it had the night before. Explosives had been placed and ignition wires had been run. The sight of them sent a chill through Annaleigh. The whole place was rigged, ready to blow at any moment.

She swallowed. She had to get Vasmir out of here, no matter what it required of her. She could not let him die. And not just because he was the last existing creation of her grandfather's. Vasmir had saved her life. She owed him the same.

She began the long trek up the many, many flights of stairs. It was somewhat easier this evening without the weight of her camera equipment. But her heart was heavy that this old place was about to come down.

Getting Vasmir free was making her nervous, too. What if the kiss didn't work? She hadn't exactly had a lot of practice in that area. She'd had boyfriends, but none of them had stuck around very long. They'd all had their reasons. She wasn't ambitious enough. She wasn't their type, whatever that meant. She read too many books. She had no money.

She was fine being alone. Mostly. She'd come to terms with it for sure. Wasn't like there was much room at her place for company anyway. Although she imagined that was about to be tested.

Vasmir would need a place to stay, unless there was some kind of halfway house for recently turned-human gargoyles, but that seemed unlikely.

Step after step, she climbed. She ran a few, eager to see him, but by the time she reached the observation deck, it was completely dark outside. She shoved the door open with her shoulder. It always stuck. She propped it open with a chunk of broken concrete and glanced behind her, praying no one had followed her tonight.

The stairwell looked and sounded empty. Good.

She took a few steps out into the open. "Vasmir? I'm here."

She went around to the part of the observation deck where his statue could be seen. She gasped. There was nothing there. He was gone. A pit opened up inside of her. Someone had taken him. She sucked in a breath and put her hand to her mouth. "Oh no."

A rush of wind filled the observation deck behind her. "What is wrong?"

She turned to see Vasmir. "I thought—you were gone and—where were you?"

"I am sorry if I frightened you." He looked genuinely

upset. "I wanted to fly. I thought I would be back before you returned."

She smiled. "It's okay. You're here now and that's what matters. We have to get you out of here. The building has been prepped for demolition." She didn't want to tell him about the explosives. It felt like a lot for him to bear.

He nodded. "I saw the men working today. They were very busy."

She moved closer to him, so happy that nothing had happened to him. "So, um, I just kiss you and you can become human?" Like a frog prince. She laughed at the thought, but his face filled with dubious curiosity at her response. "I'm not laughing at you, I swear. Just having a silly thought is all."

He tipped his head. "You find this ridiculous."

"No, no. I find it...fascinating." She slid her hand up his arm, reveling in the hard smoothness of him. "Intriguing." Her hand went farther, over the massive roundness of his shoulder until she had to come up on her tiptoes to cup his jaw. "Unbelievable." He was stone beneath her fingers and yet not without some give. Like leather. Cool, supple leather over exquisitely carved marble.

He leaned into her hand like the great cat he'd been carved after, nuzzling her palm, then sighed softly. "I will not look like this when I am human."

"You won't? What will you look like?" Her other hand

found its way to his chest. In the short time she'd been touching him, he'd warmed considerably.

He shook his head without displacing her hand. "I do not know."

She pulled her hands away. "Will you be able to change back?"

"Yes." He glanced at her hands. "Do you fear you will not find me pleasing in human form? Or is it this form you wish not to see again?"

"No, neither. Just curious." She bit her lip, then shoved away the embarrassment heating her skin. One more day and he would cease to exist when the building came down. She was not going to let that happen. "I like the form you're in very much. I always have. Ever since I was a little girl and I dreamed of...of..." *Just say it.* "Flying with you."

His lips parted and his eyes held a strange light.

She turned away. Why had she said that? Obviously, he didn't want to go carting her around like some mythological tour guide. "Forget I said anything."

"No. I will not forget it. I would...*love* to take you flying."

She glanced up through a curtain of hair. "You would? You don't think it's silly?"

He went down on one knee and his wings unfurled. "Consider me your chariot."

"Could I take pictures? Because some aerial shots would just be amazing."

"Whatever you desire."

Barely muzzling a squeal, she clapped her hands over her grinning mouth before thrusting them victoriously into the air. "Cool!"

He didn't smile back.

She dropped her hands. With one knee down, he was at eye level. "Are you sure you want to do this? You don't seem happy about it."

His brows furrowed. "I am very pleased to do this. More pleased that you would want to share this with me."

"So gargoyles don't smile then?"

He dropped his head. "I do not think you would find my smile...pleasant."

She planted her hands on her hips. "Show me."

He lifted his chin. "You are sure?"

"Yes."

Clearing his throat, he smiled.

*Holy crap.* Now she knew what a gazelle must feel like in its last moments of life. "Wow. You have a lot of teeth."

The smile vanished. "I knew you would not like it."

"No, no. I like it." She did. Knowing that he wanted to protect her made that smile wickedly delicious. "It's kind of ferocious, but as long as you're on my side, I'm okay with that."

"I will always be on your side, Annaleigh." He extended his hand. "The night sky awaits."

No one had been on her side in a long time and now that someone was, she was in danger of losing him. Forever. The thought emboldened her. She stepped forward and placed her hands on his shoulders "Don't you want your kiss?"

His throat pulsed with a swallow. "If you are willing. But there is something else I must tell you. Once you kiss me, I will be bound to you. I am already bound to do your bidding because you called me, but once turned, I will be unable to part from you for a full turning of the world."

"You mean one year?"

He nodded. "If that is too much, I understand."

"It's not too much." She hadn't been counting on a whole year. But she couldn't say no now. His time was nearly up. "Just so you understand, my apartment is tiny. I mean *tiny*. I sleep in a loft that overlooks the rest of the studio. I'm not even sure you'll fit through the door."

He dropped his other knee to the ground. That put him eye to eye with her. "There is no room for me."

"Hey, I didn't say that." There was barely room for her. "I have a couch. That's pretty much all the furniture that fits in the place, but you're welcome to it. We'll figure it out. I am *not* letting you get destroyed with the building. No matter what that means."

The corners of his mouth lifted slightly. "You are a good person, Annaleigh. You remind me of my maker."

"Did you actually know my grandfather?"

"I did."

"Wow."

"I will tell you all about him. Everything I can remember. If you wish it."

"I do. But first, let's get you free."

"You would kiss me now?"

She took a breath. "I would."

Heart pounding, she leaned in and pressed her lips to his, expecting his mouth to be hard and cold, despite the supple warmth of his shoulders beneath her hands. His mouth was nothing like she'd expected.

Pliant heat met her tentative kiss, encouraged her, welcomed her. She slanted her mouth across his, stroking her tongue over the firm seam of his lips.

A subtle tremor shook him. A low groan followed. Then his lips parted to let her in.

He tasted of sun and sky and wind. Her hands slid upward to cradle his broad jaw and she leaned in further, her body against his. Hard and muscled, he was infinitely reassuring. She could stay like this for a long, long time. Something soft and smooth hugged her. She opened her eyes. He'd wrapped his wings around her.

His hand came to rest on her hip, the heavy expanse of it radiating heat into her skin. He held her with a possessiveness she'd never felt before. The wash of sensation spilled a mewl of pleasure from her and she clung to him.

He shuddered again, then jerked back like he'd been shocked. His head dipped, his hands braced against the tiles. Great breaths expanded his frame, bowing his back until he looked more and more like the great cat he'd been carved after.

"Are you okay?" Was he about to change into his

human form? She stepped back to give him room for whatever was happening.

He nodded, picked his head up. "I am fine." Lifting himself back to one knee, he looked out at the darkening sky. "We should fly now."

# CHAPTER EIGHT

Vasmir braced himself. He could feel the power of her kiss coursing through him. The change had already begun in him, but it would not be complete until the sun rose.

The idea of being human was a heady thought. Tonight, instead of returning to his spot on the edge of the building, he would be with she who called him. He would be free.

"I'm ready," Annaleigh said.

He went to all fours and held still while she climbed gingerly on to his back. She had nothing to fear. No harm would ever come to her again.

"Great Grandpa Walters certainly had a working knowledge of human and animal musculature, didn't he? There's not a spot on you that isn't rock hard." She laughed softly. "And I don't mean because you're carved of it. It's like you're made of muscle."

"He who carved me was a talented man."

She fit herself to him, straddling the narrowest part of his waist, knees bent so that her feet hooked over the curve of his hamstrings. "Which is why his work should be preserved. I just wish I could have convinced the historical society of that."

"The bottom of my right foot bears his mark."

Her hands flattened against his shoulder blades, and he could feel her twisting to look. "You bear his mark?"

"I do. Stone carvers put their mark on all their work, but in a hidden place, usually where stone will meet stone. The maker's mark, as it is named, is only for their eyes and the eyes of the commissioner of the piece."

"I don't know why it never occurred to me that you'd have one." The words came out breathy and soft. "There is it. The star. A very ornate one. All my life I've seen that mark in my family and felt like it was something important. And look..." She hopped off his back and came to stand in front of him, where she tugged up the leg of her pants, exposing a delicate ankle, partially hidden by her sock. But above it was something he knew well. "I even had the star tattooed on me."

She who called him bore the same mark he did. His heart swelled in his chest. Surely this was a sign. Their paths were always meant to intertwine. He nodded, the best he could do with such solemn pride burning his eyes. "It is more becoming on you."

"Nah, it looks great on you." She smiled and shrugged. "But it's pretty cool we both have it, don't you think?"

"It is very...cool."

She returned to her spot on his back and settled in. The heat from her body seeped into him, giving him more strength than what he normally gathered from the sun. More strength and something new—a sense of longing. To be human, like her. When they returned from flying, he would take human form for the first time. The anticipation both thrilled and unnerved him. He twisted his head to look at her. "Are you secure?"

"Yes." She exhaled. "Also, a little nervous, but ready."

"You have nothing to fear." He shifted his weight to raise one arm and point to the building's edge. "You could fall from this height, and I would still catch you before you touched the ground." He put his hand down. She did not seem convinced. "I am very fast, very strong, and very agile."

"Like a cat," she added.

"Yes, like a cat."

"Good to know." She patted his back. "Just be gentle, okay?" Her tentative laugh filled his pointed ears. "I'm a little scared. Excited, too, but like I said nervous."

"I would never do anything to hurt you."

She nodded. "I know. I trust you."

"Hold on." Her trust in him would not be misplaced. He turned his face back toward the night sky.

Her hands clamped over his shoulders.

His muscles coiled. He went up onto his toes. A second later, he sprang into the air, his wings snapping out to catch the updrafts from the streets below.

She shrieked and threw herself flat against him, her arms wrapping around his neck. "I can't look," she said into his ear.

"You should," he said. "The city is beautiful below."

He felt her move slightly, then her breath was on his neck.

"Wow," she breathed out. "It's amazing. And you get to see this all the time. Flying or not."

"Yes. But never have I been able to share it with anyone." There was pleasure in that. And some pride, that he was able to do this for her. To give something back to she who had called him. She who had kissed him and set him free.

He took her all over the city, heading south toward the downtown area. He took his time, circling a few times over the most interesting spots. Once he'd reached the tip of the island, he curved around and returned north along the river.

"It's so beautiful from up here."

"We can fly any time you want. Are you warm enough?"

"It's a little breezy, but I'm all right."

To him that meant she was cold but didn't want to tell him. He lifted one wing slightly, adjusting his direction to take them back to the hotel. Then a thought came to him. "We do not need to return to the hotel, if you do not wish it."

"There isn't really anything I need there. And it's probably not the safest place for either of us. Where would you land instead?"

"There is a large grassy area up ahead."

"You mean Central Park?"

"I do not know its name, but if that is the green land ahead, then yes."

"Sounds good. So long as there's a spot where no one will see you."

"I will find one." He decreased his altitude by a hundred feet and scanned the swathe of green ahead of them. There were a few areas full of people, some with only a scattering, but not many that had none.

He circled, dropping lower, and found a place. A narrow strip of brown land in one of the more wooded areas. It would work nicely, although he would have to be careful of his wings. It would be a good spot to make his human transition, as well. He slowed and descended. Pulling his wings in too soon would result in a hard landing. He did not want to do that to Annaleigh.

At the last possible moment, he tucked his wings and stretched out his feet. "Hold on." He skidded to a stop, leaving two tracks behind him in the mulch and leaves, but the landing was not as rough as he had anticipated. "Are you all right? That was not as smooth as it would have been in an open field."

"I'm fine. As soon as you tucked your wings, I had a feeling we'd land a little hard." She slid off and smiled at him. "You did great finding a spot."

"Thank you."

"We have a long way to go to get back to my apartment, but I have a couple subway tokens."

He paused. "I...did not think about that. I could find a place closer and take you there."

"No, it's fine. Normally, I wouldn't ride the subway after dark, but we'll be together so it's no big deal." Her smile got a little bigger. "Unless you look like you do now. Then someone might say something." She laughed. "Then again, in this city you'd be surprised at what passes for normal."

"I am going to take on my new form. The one you made possible." He lifted his chin slightly. "I am going to become human."

She stepped back. "I can't wait."

He did not have the same anticipation. He was somewhat concerned about his human appearance. But it had to be an improvement over his countenance now, did it not? He would soon find out.

Annaleigh was not good at hiding what she was feeling. Her face was very expressive. He would know what she thought as soon as she saw him.

"Do you need more room?" She asked. "I have no idea what this entails."

"No, you are fine." He took a breath. "I can feel the change awaiting my command. I suppose all I must do is give myself to it and it will happen."

She nodded, watching him closely.

He closed his eyes and found the energy inside him. It had taken root with her kiss and had been building since then. *I am ready to be human.*

The change happened almost immediately, crackling over his skin like an icy gust of northern wind. He shivered as his body morphed into something different. His talons retracted, his teeth shortened, his bones and skin and muscles shifted. Every inch of him adapted to his new form.

"Oh," Annaleigh said softly.

He opened his eyes and looked down at himself. His body seemed normal and not much different than the one he'd had before. His wings were gone. He could sense that just from the lack of weight on his back.

He was dressed in a brown suit that reminded him of something his maker might have worn. Brown leather boots covered his feet. He stretched out his hands. His talons were gone, replaced by short, ragged fingernails.

He hesitated to look at Annaleigh, reluctant to read her expression. He decided not to, just yet. "Am I satisfactory?"

She exhaled. "Vasmir, you are very satisfactory." She laughed softly. "You're as beautiful transformed as you were a gargoyle. How do you feel?"

He looked up. She was smiling, her eyes full of happy light.

He exhaled with relief. Then smiled at the fact he was breathing. That was new. All of this was new. And wonderful. "I feel good. And very happy."

# CHAPTER NINE

By the time they reached her apartment, Annaleigh was out of steam. It had been a long few days without a lot of sleep and she was still sore from the altercation at the hotel. She was ready for bed.

Of course, she'd have to get Vasmir settled, but that shouldn't take too long. Wasn't like showing him around would take much time.

They'd stopped at the bodega on the corner and bought him a toothbrush. He'd looked longingly at a bag of salt and vinegar potato chips, so she'd bought those too, along with a prepackaged ham and cheese sub, a pint of ice cream, and a large bottle of Coke.

He had to be hungry. Not only had he probably never eaten anything in his life, but he'd exerted a lot of energy with all that flying and transforming.

She unlocked the door to her apartment and went in, flipping the switch to turn on the lights. "This is it."

He came in behind her, looking around. "This is where you live?"

"Yep. Not much too it, I'm afraid."

He walked toward the windows and turned slowly. His gaze stopped on the loft. "And that is where you sleep?"

"It is."

"And I will sleep..." He looked at the couch, pointing to it. "Here?"

She nodded, setting the grocery bag down on the small countertop. "I hope that's okay."

"It's very good."

"That suit won't be comfortable for you to sleep in, but fortunately for you, my last boyfriend left a change of clothes here and never came back for them."

"You have a *boy* friend? He will not like me being here, I think."

"Doesn't matter what he thinks, he's long gone, which is just fine with me. Anyway, it's just sweatpants and a T-shirt, but they should work pretty well as pajamas." She'd have to get him some other clothes soon. The suit he had on was old-fashioned and would make it hard for him to blend in.

Harder. He wasn't much smaller as a human than he had been as a gargoyle. He was well over six foot, broad shouldered, and angelically handsome. His mane of sandy blond hair nearly reached his shoulders, and his eyes were a captivating mossy green with glints of gold.

She had to remind herself *not* to stare at him. "I'll change in the bathroom, which is that door back there, and get myself ready for bed, then you can have it, all right?"

He nodded but looked a little confused.

"I mean so you can change in there and brush your teeth and whatever else you want to do. You can take a shower, if you like."

"A shower?"

She smiled. She'd been explaining things to him since they got on the subway, including why the guy at the other end of the car had pink hair. "Actually, why don't you change first, then you can sit on the couch and eat your dinner?"

"Are you going to eat?"

She was hungry. She nodded. "I am. But I have a microwave dinner to heat up."

His eyes narrowed.

"It's a frozen meal that goes into a special box which heats it up very quickly." She put her hand on the microwave. "Never put anything metal in here."

"I do not think I will use it at all."

She chuckled as she got out a frozen meal. Spaghetti and meatballs, one of her favorites. She peeled the film back, put it in to cook, then set the time and hit start. "I'll get you those clothes."

The small duffel bag had been sitting on the top shelf of her tiny closet for nearly two years. She got the bag down and unzipped it, pulling out the contents. "Here you go. Sweatpants, a T-shirt, socks, and sneakers that I should probably throw away. Although they don't look like they're in such bad shape."

She glanced at Vasmir's feet. They looked bigger than

the sneakers in the bag. "The sneakers are probably too small for you but the clothes should fit. Blain was close to your size." She set the clothing on the couch. "Don't worry, they're clean."

"Thank you."

She shrugged. "Thank Blain."

"I meant for all you have done for me. I am...beyond grateful. I will never be able to repay you."

"You don't have to. You saved my life." She looked up at him in time to see a tear form at the corner of his eye. She put her hand on his arm. His show of emotion was so sweet and touching. "I'm very happy that you're here and that it all worked out. Don't worry about repaying me. I consider us even."

The tear slipped down his cheek and fell, but as it fell it bounced off the throw rug covering her living room floor.

Tears did not bounce. She crouched down and picked up the little crystalline drop off the rug. It was hard. She turned the pea-sized gem in her fingers, watching as it caught the light and sent out little fiery sparks. "What on earth is this? Because it looks like a diamond."

"Yes," Vasmir said. "Gargoyle tears turn to diamonds."

She stared at him. "Seriously? You cry diamonds."

"All gargoyles do. I assume it was why those men were trying to steal my brothers. To bring them to life and cause them to weep."

Annaleigh's mouth came open, but for a few moments, she had no response.

Vasmir picked up the clothing off the couch. "You should keep that. Or perhaps, sell it. There will be some money to be had from it, for sure. Gargoyle diamonds are perfect. Flawless and without color. I will change now."

"Okay."

He went off to the bathroom.

She sat on the couch and turned on the lamp that rested on the small table next to the seating area. She held the diamond in the light and had a better look. To her naked eye, it definitely seemed perfect.

Diamonds weren't such an unusual thing for her to deal with at the shop. People brought them in to sell all the time. The shop did a fair business in estate jewelry. A diamond like this, unset and so clean, ought to bring in a few thousand dollars. More than a few, maybe. Would Mr. Tidwell let her sell it without the usual commission rate?

Probably not. But any money would come in handy. Vasmir needed clothing and her food bill would definitely go up.

The microwave beeped that her food was ready. She wrapped the diamond in a tissue, then tucked it into the zippered pocket of her purse. She'd find out tomorrow.

# CHAPTER TEN

While Vasmir slept, Annaleigh put on her best dress and arrived early for work. They'd had a long discussion last night about how things worked in the apartment, and she'd showed him how to use the TV remote since it was probably best he didn't go out until she returned.

Getting to work early was important. She needed Mr. Tidwell in a good mood. She let herself into the shop with her key, but left the lights off so that no one would think they were open just yet. She turned off the alarm with her code, then went straight to the kitchen to make coffee.

He was always happier when he didn't have to make the coffee himself. As she got it brewing, she heard the front door open again. Mr. Tidwell, no doubt. Franklin Fuller, his personal assistant, came in an hour after the boss did. Mr. Tidwell liked to have an hour alone in the morning to get ready for the day.

Annaleigh pushed the button to start the coffee brewing. She had no idea what he did during that hour, and she didn't care. It was sixty minutes of alone time for both of them and it worked for her.

Franklin, who was the son of one of Mr. Tidwell's important friends, was all right. He was young and eager and did Mr. Tidwell's bidding like a puppy dog trying to please his master. A yes man, her father would have called him.

Although he'd always been very nice to her. Even commiserating with her over the loss of her grandfather's work on the old hotel. He'd said he'd tried to get his father involved, to appeal to the historical society, but that had never amounted to anything.

She appreciated the attempt all the same.

She was about to go out onto the sales floor to greet him when she realized Mr. Tidwell was on the phone. She didn't want to interrupt him, but she also didn't want him to think she was eavesdropping. The hot water began to run through the grounds. She reached for the kitchen door, but then some of his conversation filtered in and she hesitated.

"Well, someone got the last one." He sounded angry and frustrated. "No, those two never showed up which is just as well because I would have—" He stopped talking. "Is someone here?"

With a big smile on her face, she pushed the door open. "Good morning, Mr. Tidwell. Coffee's on. I'm going to do a walk through and make sure everything's in order, then I'll clean all the glass cases."

He blinked like he was surprised to see her. "Oh, uh, very good, Annaleigh. Thank you."

"You're welcome." She took off for the back of the shop. She did not need him upset with her today. Better to give him some privacy and let him finish his call.

Once he had a free moment, she'd show him the diamond and see if he'd give her an employee discount on the standard commission. In her head, she was already allocating the money. At least a third of it would go toward Vasmir's much needed wardrobe.

Winter would be here in a few months, and he'd need some warmer things, and a good coat. Probably boots too. Gloves and a hat weren't a bad idea either.

Then she'd set aside at least two months' worth of rent. That would give her some breathing room. By then, Vasmir would have found a job. The rest would all be for living expenses. Food and electricity, mostly.

Saving a little would be nice, too, but she knew how fast money went. Especially in this city.

She straightened one of the paintings in the gallery, a pretty pastoral setting with a small cottage and few sheep dotting the hillside. She stared at it. Was staying in the city a bad idea? Maybe Vasmir would be better off in the country. Maybe they both would be.

But what would she do for work? Her degree was in art history. Not a lot of call for that in the more rural parts of the country.

She was looping back around to clean the cases when

Mr. Tidwell appeared in her path, a cup of coffee in his hand. She stopped what she was doing.

"Coffee's good," he said. "I appreciate you coming in early."

Her brows lifted. She had no poker face. "Thanks. I was sort of hoping I could have a quick chat with you." She quickly added, "I have something I'm thinking of selling." Mostly so he wouldn't think she was going to ask him for a raise.

"Oh? Well, I'll be in my office. Come in when you're ready."

"Okay. Thank you. I'll just be a few more minutes."

She cleaned the cases, which were already pretty clean, then grabbed her purse and went to his door. She knocked. "It's me."

"Come in."

He had paperwork on his desk, but he closed the folder he'd been going through. "So. You have something of value, do you? Something of your grandfather's?"

Her family history was partially what had gotten her this job. She knew that. She didn't mind it. But his referencing it made her suddenly think of an angle for the diamond. A little story to go with it so that Mr. Tidwell wouldn't question where she'd gotten it. "Something of my grandmother's, actually."

"Is that so?"

"Yes." She pulled the tissue-wrapped diamond from her purse and carefully opened it, took the diamond out, and set it on his desk. "I've had it a while. Saving it for a rainy day, you know? But then it occurred to me that maybe it's always raining." She smiled to soften the words because they sounded more pitiful than she'd meant them to.

He nodded, but his eyes on the stone. "A diamond."

She stayed quiet. He was talking to himself, anyway.

He took out a little velvet tray. She put the stone on it. He got out his jeweler's loop and fixed it to his eye, then picked up the stone with a pair of gem tweezers. He turned on his desk lamp and examined the diamond. "This is an exceptional piece. Looks like at least an IF clarity and D color."

She nodded. "That's what my grandmother always told me about it. That it was the finest diamond available for the money that had been spent on it."

He looked up at her, one eye still hidden behind the loop. "Do you know what she paid?"

"Not a clue." Annaleigh felt the sudden need to embellish. "It might have been a gift from one of her beau's. She had a lot of them back in the day."

"And you want to sell this?"

"I'm thinking about it."

He went back to looking at the stone, turning it slightly. "It's a carat at least, but probably more like a carat fifteen or a carat twenty. Nice stone. Very nice." He set the tweezers down carefully. "A diamond of this grade fetches a premium. They're rare."

She nodded like that was something she hadn't already known.

"We could easily ask twelve thousand for this stone. I have a few customers in mind already. If you're serious."

She sucked in a breath. That was more than she'd guessed. She did her best to keep cool. He loved to make customers happy. She needed to use that to her advantage. "I suppose it would all depend on how much commission I'd have to pay."

He smiled his syrupy smile. "Annaleigh, you're a valuable employee. I'm sure we could work out a deal. Employees always get a discount. You know that."

She didn't know that, because to her knowledge, it wasn't always true. The standard commission rate was thirty-five percent. She quickly did the math. She did not want to give him forty-two hundred dollars. "What would the percentage be, then?"

"I think twenty-five would be reasonable, don't you?"

She shrugged. "I guess." She reached for the stone. "I think I'll wait on selling it."

"How about twenty percent?"

She left the diamond where it was. "I thought the employee discount was half the standard rate?" She thought no such thing. She just didn't want to pay him such a big chunk of money.

"Seventeen and a half?" He mused that over.

She ran the numbers in her head. That would give him twenty-one hundred and her ninety-nine hundred. Almost ten grand. She could live with that. It would provide her and Vasmir with a lot of cushion. "You really think you have a customer for this?"

He nodded. "I'm sure of it."

"I want ten thousand dollars. Anything above that is yours."

He exhaled and sat back. "I had no idea you were capable of driving such a hard bargain. Well done, Miss Walters. Perhaps I should start bringing you in on negotiations."

She doubted that would ever happen. She smiled and picked up the diamond. "Thank you. When Franklin comes in I'll have him log the stone into inventory." She started for the door, but paused before leaving. "How soon do you think you can sell it?"

He took a moment. "I have to make a few calls, of course, but possibly the end of the day."

Annaleigh took a deep breath to keep from squealing. "Okay. Sounds good."

Mr. Tidwell's eyes narrowed. "You don't have any more of those diamonds, do you?"

She hesitated. She might have more in the future. "My grandmother had a deep jewelry box but I'm not sure there's anything else I'm ready to part with."

He nodded. "I understand. But if you do..."

"I'll be sure to let you know."

He smiled. "Thank you. Close that door, will you? I want to get started on these calls right away."

"Sure." She went back to work, her day made. Things

were about to get good for her and Vasmir. All thanks to him, obviously.

Diamond tears. She shook her head in amazement. Who would have thought such a thing could be real? Then again, she'd seen stone come to life.

Nothing seemed impossible anymore.

# CHAPTER ELEVEN

Vasmir woke with dreams still lingering in his head. Dreams of flying and Annaleigh. Good dreams. He smiled thinking about them. Sunlight poured through the windows of the apartment, casting everything in a golden glow.

He got up and stretched, then folded the blanket Annaleigh had provided for him and set it on top of the pillow she'd also given him.

Annaleigh was a wonderful person. She had shown him all sorts of things in the apartment last night. How to turn things on and off, like the lights, the shower, kitchen and bathroom faucets, and the television. How to operate the microwave, although he was still not sure about using that. How the refrigerator had to be kept shut after you took something out. Where food was. How to make cereal and toast for breakfast.

His stomach rumbled thinking about food. It was interesting to be hungry. It made him feel very human, and that made him smile. But first he went into the bathroom and looked at himself in the mirror. He'd looked at himself last night, too, but his new face took some getting used to.

Annaleigh said he was handsome. He looked at his face, trying to determine why that was. He bared his teeth. They were so blunt now. So human. He did not see what she saw, but he was happy she found him pleasing.

He took out a bowl from the cabinet, a spoon from the drawer, then a box of cereal from a different cabinet. The box had a tiger on it. He hoped the cereal was not actually made from tigers. That didn't seem appetizing.

He got milk from the refrigerator, making sure to close the door. He put cereal in the bowl, tasting one piece before doing anything else. It was sweet and crunchy, with no discernable tiger flavor.

He poured milk over the pieces, then returned the milk to the refrigerator. He carried his bowl and spoon back to the couch. He set them down on the table in front of it and used the remote to turn on the television just as she'd instructed him, pressing the power button.

An image appeared. Two people behind a desk, a blond woman and a dark-haired man. They were talking about things happening in the city.

"After nearly a hundred years since it was first constructed, the old Albemarle Hotel is set for demolition today," the man said. "We'll be taking you there live in just a few moments." He touched his ear. "Looks like our Action Nine drone is up and that feed is ready now."

The hotel appeared on the screen. It looked old and forgotten.

Vasmir sat transfixed, his breakfast ignored. His once proud home would soon be gone. It was uncomfortable to see it displayed for all the world like this, but he could not bring himself to change the channel the way Annaleigh had showed him.

His heart ached, not just for the loss of his past, but for the loss of his brothers. His throat constricted as the man on the television continued to talk about the hotel's history. When he mentioned the stonework and the famous gargoyles, Vasmir broke down.

He wished Annaleigh was here with him. Her presence always made him feel better.

The man began to count along with a clock shown on the bottom corner of the screen. When it reached zero, for a moment, nothing happened.

Then clouds of smoke and debris erupted from various floors of the hotel and it began to sink towards the earth. It collapsed slowly at first, then it fell with a rush. Plumes of dust built around it until that was all that was visible.

The hotel was gone. Reduced to rubble. He'd known it was going to happen, but seeing it cut through him. He wept until he had no more tears left.

Annaleigh had not expected to come home with a check, and yet there was one in her purse. Her steps were light and her heart full. This money was exactly what they needed. And Mr. Tidwell had promised to sell any other diamonds she brought him with the same speed and profit.

She couldn't wait to tell Vasmir. She'd cash the check on her lunch break tomorrow, then on Saturday, they would go shopping and buy him everything he needed. It was exciting.

Feeling like doing something special, she stopped on the way home and picked up a pizza with extra pepperoni. Vasmir seemed like a meat eater. She carried it up to the apartment almost buzzing with excitement.

She unlocked the door, happy that he'd kept it locked like she'd asked him to, and went inside. He was standing by the windows, looking out, but turned as she came in. She put the pizza on the counter. "How was your day?"

He looked miserable. "The hotel is gone. My home, my brothers..." He sighed heavily. "It was all on the television."

"Oh, Vasmir. I'm so sorry." She put her purse alongside the pizza and went to him. She gave him a hug. "That had to have been so hard to watch. It hurts me, too, to know that it's gone. All of that work done by my grandfather."

If she'd known it was going to be televised, she never would have shown him how to use the TV. She looked up at him. "But at least you survived."

A hint of a smile played across his face. "Yes. Thanks

to you." He touched her hair. "I am done being sad. You are home. I feel better already."

She smiled. "I feel better, too. And I have some great news."

He looked toward the kitchen. "Is the news about that delicious smell?"

A laugh bubbled up before she could answer him. "No, that's pizza. It's our dinner. The news is I sold the diamond. For a *lot* of money. We're going shopping for you on Saturday. You'll have all the clothing you need."

"That is good news. I do not want to be a burden to you."

She took hold of his hands. "You're not. Please don't ever think of yourself that way. You're not a burden. At all. You just gave me a diamond! That money will mean a lot for us. Okay?"

"Okay."

She wanted to kiss him again, but wasn't sure how he'd feel about that. Maybe the only kiss he wanted from her was the one he'd already gotten. "Are you hungry?"

He nodded. "Yes."

"I'll get some plates and bring the pizza over." Normally, she would have changed after work, but the pizza would only stay hot for so long.

"I can help."

"Okay, you get the plates. I'll get napkins and the pizza."

They worked together to set up their dinner on the coffee table. She got them each a glass of water, then found a show about animals that she thought he might like. They sat on the couch. She opened the box. "This is pepperoni pizza."

She put a slice on each of their plates.

He watched how she picked hers up and imitated her. His eyes widened as he took his first bite. "This is *good*."

She smiled. "Yeah, I love pizza. I don't eat it that often because it's cheaper to make something, but I thought we should have a treat tonight."

"You have reminded me of something." He got up and walked over to the small table beside the couch. He picked up a bowl that was sitting there, one of the small white kind she used for ice cream sometimes. He handed it to her. "I was sad today, as I told you. Also, gargoyles are very emotional creatures. We do not hide our feelings well. But this should mean we can have pizza whenever we want."

She gaped at the contents of the bowl. It was full of diamonds.

# CHAPTER TWELVE

"All right," Annaleigh said. "You convinced me to let go of one more. This one is a bit more special."

Mr. Tidwell practically panted with eagerness. He got out his loop and tweezers. "Is that so?"

She nodded as she unwrapped the gem. "It's got the faintest wash of pink to it."

"Pink?" His brow furrowed. "Are you sure? Pink diamonds are very rare and that color in the same quality would mean a much bigger price."

She set the stone down in front of him, leaving it on the white tissue to really show off the color. "Well, it's not quite as large as the last one."

He gasped at the stone. "I would say that's more than a faint hint of pink. I believe that would qualify as Fancy Intense. The stone looks to be a little shy of carat."

He shook his head as he looked at her. "This might easily fetch..." He swallowed. "Fifty thousand dollars."

Her mouth fell open. Her heart beat faster. "What?" That was an unimaginable sum.

Mr. Tidwell changed the subject as he picked up the

stone with his tweezers and looked at it through his loop. "Your grandfather was a bricklayer?"

"Stonemason and master sculptor," she corrected him.

"And he earned enough money doing that to buy stones like this for your grandmother?" Mr. Tidwell's eyes had narrowed, and he seemed to be thinking hard.

Annaleigh quickly did the same thing, coming up with what she hoped was a credible explanation. "Family history says he worked for many very wealthy clients, one of whom paid him in loose gems."

His squint remained, like he was trying to comprehend what she'd told him. "And you inherited them all?"

She did some more fast thinking. "Only two others, both smaller, more ordinary stones that I don't think I'll be parting with."

In truth, the bowl Vasmir had handed her last night had contained at least twenty-five diamonds of various shapes and colors. But Mr. Tidwell was asking a lot of questions. Lesson learned. The next stone she sold would be through someone else.

Although if she got fifty thousand dollars for this one, it would be a while before she sold another. Unless... maybe moving to the country wasn't such a bad idea after all. If she sold a few more of the colored diamonds, they might even have enough to buy a house.

Her mind swept her away imagining their new life in a different place. Vasmir could fly as much as he wanted in the country.

"Annaleigh. *Annaleigh?*"

She blinked. "Sorry. My train of thought got the best of me. What did you say?"

"I was asking if you were serious about selling this stone?"

"Yes, absolutely."

"Are you in some kind of trouble that you need money?"

That seemed like an awfully personal question. She did her best to smile. "No. Just thought it would be nice to have a little nest egg, is all. These stones haven't been doing anything but sitting around, being unappreciated. Might as well go to someone who will enjoy them, right?"

"Right," Mr. Tidwell said slowly. He looked at the diamond again, then made a few notes on the pad by his elbow.

Did he believe her? She wasn't sure. She also didn't really care. All he had to do was broker the sale. "So do you know anyone who might be interested in such a stone?"

"I do. This might take a little more time than the first stone."

"That seems reasonable." She put her hand on the desk like she was about to wrap the diamond up again and decided to dangle a carrot to keep him honest. Or as honest as Mr. Tidwell was capable of being. "You know, if this one sells for a good price, I *might* be persuaded to let the blue one go, too."

His eyes widened. "You have a blue diamond?"

She nodded innocently. "Not quite as dark as the Hope Diamond, but similar. A little bigger than this pink one. It's very pretty."

He rubbed at his chin. "I'll do my best to get you a great price on the pink."

She picked up the stone. "Then I'll have Franklin log it in."

"Wonderful." He picked up his phone.

She closed his office door without being asked.

He still hadn't emerged by lunch time. She'd seen Franklin go in twice with fresh cups of coffee and little plates of cookies. Annaleigh figured he was hard at work selling that diamond.

She ran to the bank to deposit the first check. She kept some cash out, too. The diamond had come from Vasmir. He ought to get some of the money from it. When she returned, she ate a quick lunch of instant noodles and an apple.

The rest of the day flew by, in part because she once again found herself lost in a variety of daydreams. Some about living in the country and all that might entail. Some about shopping for Vasmir.

And some about life with him. She was falling for him. She just wasn't sure he felt the same way about her. But he'd told her he would have to remain with her for a year. And a lot could happen in that amount of time.

It was nearly closing time when Mr. Tidwell came

out of his office. He had a rather satisfied look on his face. "Annaleigh, could I see you for a moment?"

"Sure." She went into his office.

He closed the door but didn't sit. "It's been quite a day. Your diamond got a lot of interest."

"That's good."

He grinned. "I can't tell you who bought it, but I can tell you that they agreed on a price of seventy-seven thousand dollars."

She sat down. "Seventy-seven."

He nodded. "The commission still needs to come out of that, you understand."

"Yes, of course."

"All things considered, I've decided to take a very small percentage. Ten percent. I think you'll agree that's more than fair."

"It is." That percentage was almost as staggering as the sale price. She would have thought he'd have wanted a good deal more. But that would leave her with a little over sixty-nine thousand dollars. An amazing amount of money.

"Thank you." She knew Mr. Tidwell had made such an uncharacteristically altruistic move to sway her into selling the other diamond she'd mentioned.

But she was starting to think her time in the city was coming to an end.

"There is one more thing," Mr. Tidwell said. "I have been very impressed with your work ethic lately. I'd like to offer you a promotion to assistant manager of the fine arts department. What do you say?"

"That's very kind of you." She had too much on her mind to answer him. She had no idea if the promotion came with more money or just more work, but she wasn't sure she was going to be here. She needed to talk to Vasmir. "Can I give you my answer tomorrow?"

"Of course. I should have the check for you tomorrow as well. The buyer is eager to get their hands on the stone and has promised a wire transfer first thing."

"That's great." She got up. "Thanks again. I guess I'll see you tomorrow."

"Oh, one more thing. I nearly forgot." He went to his desk and fished something out of the top drawer. A small envelope. "Here. In appreciation for these two sales. I realize you've made a good deal of money from them, but the goodwill we've earned making customers happy is worth a bit itself. Dinner on me. I took the liberty of making a reservation for you at seven. Not easy to come by but I pulled a few strings. It's for two so if you'd like to take a friend..."

She took the envelope. It was for a very popular restaurant called Meridian. The place was impossible to get into from what Annaleigh understood. Not that she'd ever tried. It was far too expensive for her budget. He *really* wanted that blue diamond. "This will be a real treat. Wow. Thank you very much."

"I'll see you tomorrow. Have a good night."

"You too." She smiled all the way home. She and

Vasmir would have a very nice night out. A date, if you wanted to put a name to it. Did he know what a date was? Maybe not. But first, they'd have to get him something to wear.

Thankfully, she had plenty of cash on her from going to the bank. She went into the apartment.

Vasmir had the television on, but as soon as she stepped inside, he turned it off and stood. "How was your day?"

"It was good. Really good." She explained everything from the pink diamond to the job offer and the dinner that awaited them. "We'll have to be quick. We need to get you something nice to wear."

"I could wear my suit."

"It's a little old fashioned. You need clothes anyway."

"Whatever you think."

She stayed in her work clothes, which was a black skirt with a patterned blouse, although she changed out of her flats and into low heels. She added some dangling earrings, too, and refreshed her makeup. When she came out of the bathroom, she saw the two film canisters that she'd filled with the diamonds that had been in the bowl.

The canisters were still sitting on the kitchen counter. Seemed wrong to leave them out like that, but she didn't exactly have a safe to put them in. Impulsively, she stuck them in her coat pocket.

Vasmir didn't have a coat yet, but they'd soon fix that. They went two blocks down to Herrman's

Menswear. Annaleigh had always admired the window displays. Now she had a reason to shop there.

With the salesman's help, they got Vasmir an outfit of a beautiful pair of gray dress pants, a soft cashmere sweater of marled heather blue, and gorgeous wool coat of charcoal. The salesman brought over some black leather shoes and dress socks too.

Vasmir stepped out of the dressing room, his gaze going to Annaleigh, not the mirror. "What do you think?"

She blew out a little air. What she thought was that he was the most beautiful man she'd ever seen. "You look...like a model."

The salesman nodded. "You're right. He does. Maybe we should use him in our ads." He snagged a blue scarf from one of the displays and draped it under the collar of Vasmir's coat. "There," he said, stepping back.

Vasmir's brow furrowed as he finally glanced in the mirror. "Is that good?"

Annaleigh nodded, suddenly feeling a little warmer than she had before. "It's very good." She turned to the salesman. "We'll take it. All of it."

# CHAPTER THIRTEEN

Vasmir thought his new clothes were fine. The sweater was very soft. But mostly he liked them because Annaleigh liked them.

When they arrived at the restaurant, Annaleigh spoke to someone just inside the front door, and they were ushered back to a table. The restaurant was quiet and dimly lit with candles flickering on the table and crystal sconces on the walls. White cloths draped the tables and the silver cutlery gleamed.

Without being told, he knew this was a fancy place. He would be very careful in what he did, relying on Annaleigh's actions to guide him.

They were seated and given menus, then told their server would be with them shortly. Crystal goblets of ice water were already at their places, and the delicious aromas of meat wafted from the kitchen.

Annaleigh leaned in toward him and very quietly said, "Can you read?"

He smiled. "Yes, I can read."

"Oh. I wasn't sure, but that's great."

"This dining establishment is very fancy."

"It is. And hard to get into. My boss made all the arrangements, though. He knows people. And he's paying for everything so order whatever you like."

Vasmir looked at the menu. He looked harder. Those prices seemed wrong. Or he was not reading it correctly. He leaned in toward Annaleigh, the same way she'd done to him. "It says the chicken is fifty-two dollars."

She looked at her menu. "That's right."

"How many chickens is that for?"

She snorted softly, rolling her lips in like she was trying to keep from making noise. "It's for part of a chicken."

He frowned. "Which part?"

"The meat part." She laughed. "Don't worry about the cost. Mr. Tidwell's paying. And if chicken is what you want, I'm sure it'll be good. Everything here is supposed to be done to perfection."

A server approached them, an older man in white shirt, a long black tie, black pants, and a long black apron tied around his waist. "Good evening, and welcome to Meridian. I'm Charles and I'll be taking care of you this evening. Can I get you something to drink? Some wine, perhaps? We have an extensive menu."

"That might be nice," Annaleigh said, looking at Vasmir. "What do you think?

He nodded. If she wanted something, she ought to have it. "Whatever you choose is fine with me."

She looked at the server again. "I'm not a big wine drinker but what do you recommend?"

"Are you celebrating anything? Something sparkling might be nice."

She looked at Vasmir again, the light from the candle flickering in her eyes. "We are sort of celebrating. Something sparkling sounds good. Whatever you think. We'll take a bottle. Just don't make it the most expensive. My boss is paying for this meal."

Charles smiled. "I understand. I have a sparkling red in mind that I think you'll both enjoy. As for our specials this evening, we have a tomahawk ribeye for two served with a peppercorn sauce, horseradish mashed potatoes, and baby peas, as well as a trout almandine with wild rice, and petite haricot vert."

Vasmir touched Annaleigh's arm. "You decide."

She smiled at Charles and without hesitation said, "The tomahawk ribeye."

"Excellent choice."

Vasmir thought so too.

"How would you like that cooked?"

"Medium rare," Annaleigh answered.

"Perfect." Charles took their menus. "How about some crab-stuffed mushrooms to start? They're a very popular dish."

"Sounds great," she said.

"Excellent. I'll get the order in and be right back with your wine."

As he left, Vasmir sipped his water and looked around, watching how the other diners behaved. They were all rather sedate but seemed to be enjoying themselves. He turned back to Annaleigh. "Thank you for bringing me here."

"You can thank Mr. Tidwell. I never would have been able to afford this place." She shook her head. "Now, I could. I mean, thanks to you. But not before you."

"I am pleased that I can provide you with means."

"You've provided us both with means. Which is the perfect segue into something I want to discuss." She hesitated. "What would you think about moving out of the city?"

He'd never been anywhere else. "Both of us?"

She laughed. "Yes, of course."

"Where would you have us go?"

"I was thinking somewhere in the country. If we sold a few more of the diamonds, we could afford to buy a small house on some land and have a place of our own. We'd still have to work at some kind of jobs, but I was thinking the countryside might give you more freedom. To—"

Charles returned with a bottle of wine and two glasses. Behind him was another server with a bucket on a stand. The bucket was filled with ice. "Here we are. A lovely sparkling pinot noir."

He uncorked the bottle and poured a small amount into one of the glasses, then handed it to Annaleigh.

She took a sip and smiled right away. "That's very good. I like that a lot. Good choice."

Charles nodded. "Thank you, miss." He filled both the glasses. "Your steak will be up shortly. Enjoy."

He left them. Annaleigh picked up her glass and held it out to Vasmir. "Here's to us."

He picked his glass up and held it the same way she was. She touched her glass to his, making a little clink. Then she drank, so he did too.

The wine was bubbly and sweet and went down surprisingly easy. "That is not awful."

She grinned. "It's not awful at all."

It was so good, he took another drink, this time tipping the glass back and draining it.

"Whoa," Annaleigh said. "Go easy on that. Although, you're a big guy. I suppose it'll take quite a bit to affect you."

"Affect me how?"

"Well, it's alcohol. It'll make you…" She shrugged. "Alcohol lowers your inhibitions. It can make you do things you might not normally do. Make you act not like yourself. Just be careful, is all."

He searched himself for any strange feelings, but all he felt was good. Happy. He leaned closer and kissed Annaleigh. When he was done, he straightened. "That was not because of the wine. It was because I wanted to."

She smiled. "Good to know."

Another server came by and refilled Vasmir's glass with the sparkling wine. He took another drink.

"We should get some of this to drink at your home."

Annaleigh took out her phone and tapped away at the screen. A moment later, she said, "I don't know. That stuff is fifty dollars a bottle." She grimaced. "I guess Mr. Tidwell knew this wasn't going to be a cheap dinner, but I hope that wasn't too much."

"Annaleigh?" Vasmir lifted his glass.

She looked at him. "Yes?"

"I can make more tears. Money will not be a problem." He drained his glass again. "We should get another bottle."

A small smile bent her mouth, and she took a sip of her wine, too. "I don't know. Maybe we should pay for one ourselves. It is really good. And I do have cash on me."

He nodded. "That is good."

"It is really your money. I mean, those diamonds were all your doing so..."

Charles returned. He stopped at the table and refilled Vasmir's glass again. "How are you doing? Are you enjoying the wine? Your steak is about to come out."

Vasmir lifted his glass. "We are doing well. The wine is very enjoyable. We would like another bottle." He drank a deep draught before setting it down again.

"Excellent," Charles said. "I'll be right back with that."

Vasmir felt warm and happy in a way that required no effort. He laughed softly.

Annaleigh glanced at him. "What are you laughing about?"

He shook his head. "I do not know."

She snorted. "I do. You're tipsy."

"Tipsy?" He frowned. The room seemed to tilt to one side. And his stomach twisted. He opened his mouth to breathe, trying to quell the sudden queasiness that had begun.

"You'd better slow down on the wine. Alcohol on an empty stomach hits you harder than if you've eaten something."

His happiness left him. "I do not feel well. At. All." He needed to lay down. Now.

"Oh boy. You look a little green. Hang on." She lifted her hand.

Charles returned. "What can I do for you, miss?"

"Something's come up and we need to go. Can you cancel that second bottle of wine, and box everything for us to take home?"

Charles nodded, glancing quickly at Vasmir. "Shall I call you a cab as well?"

"That would be great, thank you."

In a matter of minutes, they were headed outside to a waiting car. Annaleigh had a bag full of food. The fresh air helped Vasmir's queasiness a little.

He slumped into the car, horrified by what had happened. "I ruined the evening. I am very sorry."

Annaleigh just smiled and gave the driver her

address. "It's okay," she said softly. "Now we can eat on the couch in our pajamas."

She truly did not seem mad. But Vasmir was mad at himself. He had done something foolish and wrecked Annaleigh's night. He would make up for it. He closed his eyes.

Somehow.

# CHAPTER FOURTEEN

Annaleigh wasn't going to laugh at Vasmir's unfortunate intoxication, but it *was* amusing. She felt bad for him, not just because he felt bad, but because he thought he'd ruined the dinner.

He really hadn't. They had their food and now they could eat it at home while being comfortable on the couch. That might make it taste even better. And there was no way the effects of the wine could last much longer. He probably just needed food and a nap.

He groaned softly, then let out a deep sigh.

"How are you feeling?"

"Like I am not very smart."

She did her best to suppress a smile. "There aren't many people who haven't had a bad experience with alcohol, myself included. You'll be all right soon." She wondered if him being newly human was why the alcohol had hit him so hard, but that didn't seem like a good topic while the cab driver could hear them.

"I am never drinking wine again." He tipped his head back. "How long before everything stops spinning?"

She patted his arm. "Your body just has to process it.

You can lay down on the couch when we get in and I'll get the food ready."

"Eating does not feel like a wise decision."

"It'll actually help you, but I understand that your stomach is probably a little queasy right now."

"Yes."

"Poor baby." She patted his arm. "We'll get you all fixed up."

"I am not a baby."

She smirked. "It's just a figure of speech."

They were almost to the apartment now. A few more minutes and the cab pulled over. She paid, then helped Vasmir out, making sure she had their food.

They stood on the sidewalk for a moment. The cold air might help him, she thought. The cab had been stuffy and too warm. "How are you doing?"

He took a deep breath and seemed to look less green. "A little better, I think. But I am still ashamed."

"There's nothing to be ashamed about. I'm serious. You didn't do anything to embarrass me or yourself. The wine hit you hard. There might be something in your new…form that makes you more susceptible to it. Don't beat yourself up about it, okay?"

He slanted his eyes at her and nodded reluctantly.

She smiled. "Good. Now let's get inside, get comfortable, and enjoy the rest of our evening."

They went into the lobby and straight to the elevator.

When they stepped out onto her floor, they took a few strides toward her apartment, then Vasmir grabbed her arm and stopped them, a look of intense concentration on his face as he stared down the hall.

"What is it?"

He shook his head, lowering his voice. "That smell." His nostrils flared. "I remember it."

She inhaled, then answered in a whisper, although she wasn't sure why. "All I smell is cheap aftershave."

He lifted his head suddenly. "The men from the hotel."

Her eyes widened. "Now I remember it too." Her heart started to beat faster as the memory of that night returned. "Do you think they've found me?"

Vasmir inched along the wall toward her apartment. "Not the two I dispatched. But perhaps the third has been sent to search your home." He pointed at her door.

The lock had fresh scratches on the metal. "I should call the police."

He glanced at her. "Or I could deal with him. Find out who sent him. That is the one who must be dealt with or this will not stop."

Another reason to move to the country, she thought. "Are you going to…dispatch him too?"

Vasmir's eyes narrowed with serious intent. "If he tries to hurt you, I will do what is necessary."

Not really an answer, but she wasn't going to push the subject. "Just don't kill anyone in the apartment, okay? That will create all kinds of problems. Not to mention a mess. Also, you shouldn't really kill anyone at all. If you can help it."

"Stay behind me. I will go in first."

She gave him a thumbs up. She definitely wasn't arguing *that*. At least his intoxication seemed to be gone. Maybe he'd had a rush of adrenaline and overcome it. There was no telling how the gargoyle metabolism worked.

He put his hand on the doorknob, shot her a quick look, then opened the door and quietly slipped in.

She followed. The lights were on, and the apartment was a mess. Things everywhere, couch cushions tossed aside, cabinets open, papers strewn about. Her camera bag was open on the floor, the contents emptied out. She prayed it wasn't damaged, but that was the least of her worries now.

Vasmir didn't go any further. He just pointed up.

She nodded in understanding. Whoever was riffling through her things was upstairs in the loft. They could hear him moving things. Looking for...money? If that was his hope, he'd picked the wrong apartment.

Vasmir reached past her, quietly shut the door, then locked it. He put his hand up to indicate she should stay. Then he stepped back from her and transformed into his gargoyle form.

The man in the loft was about to get a big surprise.

Vasmir reached past her again, this time with a hand that bore long talons, curved like sickles. Shifting back to his true form had replaced the broken ones. He used a talon to flick off the lights, pitching the place into sudden darkness.

"What the—" A dull thump was followed by a louder one.

She couldn't see a thing. She squeezed her eyes shut to help them acclimate to the dark faster.

When she opened them, she could see very clearly. Vasmir was standing in the middle of the living room holding a man by the throat.

"Who sent you?" Vasmir snarled.

"What...are...you," the man choked out.

"Tell me who sent you," Vasmir repeated.

Annaleigh turned on the lamp by the couch so she could see better. "Tell him or he'll kill you."

The man's eyes widened, but that was more likely because he could now see Vasmir clearly. She glanced at him. He did look pretty scary. His teeth and talons alone were enough to put a fright into anyone. But then there were the wings and his cat-like features.

Annaleigh crossed her arms. "You were with the other two at the hotel, weren't you?"

Finally, the man looked at her. "Y-yes."

"Have you seen those two since then?"

The man hesitated. "No."

She touched Vasmir's arm. "Can he breathe? If he passes out before he can answer..."

Vasmir nodded and relaxed his grip.

Annaleigh spoke to the man again. "There's a reason you haven't seen them, and if you don't want to end up like them, you should probably tell us who hired you."

He tried to nod. "I was just supposed to find some diamonds."

"I do not believe you." Vasmir's hands tightened.

The man squawked out a noise and suddenly seemed to be deliberately *not* looking at Vasmir. "An-and look for a statue of a gargoyle."

Things were coming together in Annaleigh's head. "The same person who sent you here also sent you and your buddies to the hotel, didn't they?"

The man gave a short nod that bounced his head off Vasmir's hands. How his talons weren't slicing open any veins, she had no idea.

She sighed. "I'm tired of this conversation."

Vasmir frowned. "You are done with him?"

"No. Just done talking." She stepped forward and riffled through the man's pockets, quickly finding what she was looking for. His phone.

"Lower him a little?" She asked.

Vasmir complied.

She held the phone in front of the man's face so the lock screen unlocked. Then she tapped on the icon to look at his text messages. Her heart sank as she realized what she was seeing.

"Of course. It all makes sense now." She took a deep breath and looked at Vasmir. "I know who sent him."

# CHAPTER FIFTEEN

Vasmir blinked at that news. "You do?"

Annaleigh nodded and held the screen out to him. "Look at the initials attached to the text message."

Vasmir did not understand what the initials meant, but it was plain Annaleigh did. "I see them. What do they mean?"

"FF?" She stared at the phone again, disgust in her eyes. "It has to be Franklin Fuller, my boss's assistant. That little low life. I never would have guessed he had it in him."

The man still dangling from Vasmir's hands let out a strangled moan. Vasmir gave him a shake. "Is that who sent you? Franklin Fuller?"

A meep of terror left the man's throat. "He's got money and connections. His father is..." The words ended in a garbled sob.

Annaleigh patted Vasmir's arm. "Let him talk." Then she leaned closer. "Who? Who's Franklin's father?"

"Sebastian Fuller," the man reluctantly answered. "He runs half the city."

Annaleigh sucked in a breath. "Sebastian Fuller is a crime boss?"

The man nodded weakly.

Vasmir lowered the man until his feet touched the floor and relaxed his hands. There was nowhere for him to run if he tried. And Vasmir would take him flying if he lunged at Annaleigh. "He sent you here? Or his son?"

"His son. The kid's trying to impress his old man, make a name for himself. He wanted those gargoyles off the old Albemarle Hotel. Said they were real valuable." The man shook his head. "We couldn't get 'em off. Not in one piece. Stupid hunks of rock."

Anger churned up red hot in Vasmir's belly. He leaned toward the man. "They were not stupid hunks of rock. They were my—"

"Vasmir?"

He looked at Annaleigh, his entire being seething with rage.

"This man is not who we need to deal with."

She was right. Even so, he wanted to make the man pay.

She held his gaze. "He won't come back here. Ever." She glanced at the man. "Will you?"

"Never. Not in a million years. Not if the kid threatens my life. In fact, you know what? Imma get out of the city. Tonight. You'll never see me again and neither will he."

"He touched your things," Vasmir said, his anger slowly receding. "Destroyed some of them."

She bent to gather up her camera gear. It looked all right. Thankfully.

"I'm real sorry about that," the man interjected. "I got some money on me. You can have it, if you want. I swear, I will never bother you, or anyone, ever again."

"I don't want your money," Annaleigh said, straightening. Her eyes held a steely light Vasmir had never seen before. "But if you come back here, if I ever see you in my neighborhood, I will allow Vasmir to whatever he likes with you. And trust me, you won't escape him. Those wings aren't just for looks. Do you understand what I'm saying?"

The man whimpered and nodded.

"You won't say a word about this to anyone, either. Including Franklin. Not a word. Is that also clear?"

"Lady, no one would believe me anyway."

Vasmir had a feeling Franklin would. Few humans knew the value of a gargoyle. The truth of his kind had long ago been lost to the world, but someone had passed it down. A few stories perhaps. A tale viewed as a myth.

But interesting enough that this Franklin had decided to see if it was true.

Annaleigh reached into the man's pocket again and pulled out his wallet. She used her phone to snap photos of his identification. Arnie Calhoun. If that was his real name. Then she tucked the wallet back into his pocket. "I'm keeping your phone, Arnie."

She went into the settings and turned off facial recognition, then changed the passcode to 1234. Something easy for Vasmir. Then she looked at Arnie again. "If I get one whiff of you warning Franklin, I'll send a full report of the break-in, along with the picture of your license to the NYPD."

The man swallowed but stayed silent.

"Vasmir, throw him out of the apartment."

Vasmir smiled and the man shrank back. He grabbed the man and hauled him toward the windows.

"Nope, not that way. Through the door, please," Annaleigh added.

With a sigh, Vasmir dragged the man in the other direction. He tossed him out into the hall, then closed the door again. "You are soft-hearted."

"You mean because I let him go? Or because I was willing to kiss a gargoyle to save his life?"

Vasmir grinned at her response. "Do you know where Franklin lives?"

"I do. I had to drop some files off for Mr. Tidwell once. I knew Franklin came from money. He lives in a very nice brownstone that not many people could afford, let alone a thirty-something who works as a personal assistant. But I never guessed his father was that kind of guy."

"Are we going to pay him a visit?"

"I think we should. Right after I change." She smiled at him. "You, however, should stay just as you are."

He raised his brows. "Are we flying?"

"It would be faster."

"I am ready when you are."

"I'll just be a minute." She went up into the loft to change.

While she did that, he busied himself with putting things right in the apartment. At least as much as he remembered how they were.

When she came back down in jeans, boots, and a coat, she smiled. "Thank you, but you didn't have to do that."

"I live here, do I not? I should share responsibilities." He looked around. "And he was here because of me."

"Maybe indirectly, but he was here because I sold those diamonds through Mr. Tidwell. That's how Franklin knew. He logged those stones in, and he knew who my grandfather was. He also knew I'd been going to the hotel. I showed him a lot of the pictures I'd taken. Including those of the gargoyles. He put two and two together. *And* he's been interested in my grandfather since..." She narrowed her eyes. "Since right around the time the destruction of the Albemarle Hotel was announced, and I said something about my connection to it."

She frowned. "What a phony he was, pretending to be interested. He was, but only because he thought he could finally find out if what he knew about gargoyles was real or not. What a creep."

"I have a feeling he will soon know that gargoyles are very real. Perhaps more real than he'd hoped for," Vasmir said. "We should go to the roof. Is that possible?"

"Yes, follow me."

They left the apartment and took the elevator to the top floor, then the steps to the roof. The wind brushed past them as they emerged from the stairwell.

"Which way?" Vasmir asked.

"Upper west side. Eighty-eighth Street. Do you know the area?"

"I have flown every inch of this city many times. I know it. The home is near the large park."

"That's right. Listen, I want to go to his door alone. He'll let me in because he knows me."

"Then what?"

She took a breath. "Then we scare the living daylights out of him. Enough so that he never goes after either of us again."

Vasmir went down onto all fours so that she could climb on. "I believe I know just how to do that."

# CHAPTER SIXTEEN

She laid low along Vasmir's back, letting the wind sail over her. She hated that her home had been violated, but she'd get past that. Dealing with Franklin would help. But nothing had been taken and she'd had the diamonds on her the whole time, so they'd never been in jeopardy.

The city below was beautiful, but she was done with living here. She would go to work tomorrow, get her check for the pink diamond from Mr. Tidwell, and give him her resignation. The country had to be safer. She didn't care what she ended up doing for work.

Maybe they could find a place with enough land to have a good-sized garden. Maybe even some chickens. The country life might be just the thing.

Vasmir descended, landing in the same part of the park where they'd been previously. "This seems to be a safe spot."

She nodded and slid off. "Franklin's place is just a short walk from here. This is perfect."

He turned to see her. "I will follow you from the sky and take note of which building it is."

"The brownstone has a small backyard. You should be able to land there. There's a terrace on the sixth floor, too, but I think the backyard would be better. If you can manage it."

Vasmir nodded. "I will. Do not worry."

"Also, the back of the house is all glass so you should have a clear view of us."

"Are you going to confront him about what happened?"

"I am. I still have the burglar's phone so I can prove I know what he was up to. And I'm going to record our conversation on my phone. That will be my leverage against him."

"And if he does not comply?"

"Then you get your turn to make him see reason."

Vasmir grinned. "I can do what I like?"

His amusement was entertaining. "So long as you don't kill him or cause him permanent bodily harm. His father is not someone we want to be mad at us. No matter where we end up living."

"I understand. I will see you soon." He crouched like he was about to take off again.

"Hey."

He stopped and turned back toward her. "Yes?"

She took his face in her hands and kissed him, savoring the moment of contact. "I am very glad you're on my side."

"I am also glad of this. We are a good team."

"We are." She let him go, still smiling. "See you there."

He leaped into the sky and disappeared into the darkness. She picked her way through the trees and out onto the street, quickly getting her bearings.

She glanced up a few times but was never able to spot Vasmir. She knew he was up there, though. That gave her a lot of confidence.

There were lights on in almost every floor of Franklin's far too large brownstone. What did the power bill matter when his father was probably paying for it? Just like he'd probably paid for the brownstone itself. She'd looked the place up on a real estate app once, right after she'd first visited it. According to the app, it was worth nearly twelve million dollars.

Twelve million. And Franklin was working as a personal assistant. She should have known something was fishy with the guy then.

She knocked on his door, then turned on the record feature on her phone and tucked it into the front pocket of her purse.

Franklin appeared shortly after in a cashmere tracksuit and Gucci slippers. His brows rose for a moment like he was surprised to see her, then he laughed it off. "Annaleigh! What brings you around?"

"I was in the neighborhood. Got stood up on a date." She shrugged and gave him a sad smile. "I was feeling kind of down. I guess I just wanted to see a smiling face. I'm sorry, I shouldn't have come."

"No, no, you definitely should have. Come in. We'll have a drink and you can tell me all about the creep who stood you up."

"You're sure?"

He answered her with a megawatt smile as he opened the door wider. "I'm positive."

She stepped inside. The place smelled like the lobby of an expensive hotel she'd once been in. Not to stay, just to deliver a package for a guest there.

"You want something to drink? I was just about to make a gin and tonic, myself."

"Just the tonic would be great for me." She followed him into the living room, where a gas fire crackled away in a sealed fireplace. The entire house was done in white and the softest shades of ivory and cream. No doubt he had a cleaning crew that helped him keep it that way.

It was beautiful, but she'd have ruined the look on day one. You couldn't eat chocolate ice cream on a white couch.

He went into the kitchen, which was open to a small seating area that led out to the backyard. With all the lights on, the glass walls looked like mirrors. If Vasmir was back there, which she was sure he was, there was no way Franklin would see him.

She tried to see past the reflections, but it was impossible.

Ice tinkled in glasses and Franklin appeared at her elbow, her tonic in one hand, his mixed drink in the other. "Here you go. Let's toast to those diamonds you sold this week. You go, girl!"

She took the glass, sipped a small amount, then set it down on the coffee table. His mention of the diamonds was all the opening she needed. "That's actually why I came here tonight."

He frowned. "I don't follow. The diamonds?"

"Yes."

"You want some advice on how to spend that money? I'm your man. You know, you could use a great handbag. I will totally take you to Gucci myself. My personal shopper there, Randi, is the greatest."

She didn't smile like he probably expected. Instead, she stared directly into his eyes. He was so full of himself. And he very obviously thought he was untouchable. She walked to the big double sliders and opened them like she needed air. Vasmir was there, crouched and waiting. She turned to face Franklin again. "My apartment was broken into this evening."

He blinked and shook his head. "How awful."

"Do you really think it's awful?"

"Of course, I do."

"Then why send your goon to riffle through all of my things?"

"*My*—" He laughed. "What are you talking about?"

She glared at him. "You know exactly what I'm talking about. And exactly what he was looking for."

Franklin's smile slipped away. "Annaleigh, I really

don't know what you mean." He downed half of his gin and tonic.

She pulled out the burglar's phone. "This is the phone I took from the man I found in my house. Arnie Calhoun. Would you like me to read some of the text messages between you two? Just to refresh your memory?"

Franklin's face morphed from innocent confusion to a hard sneer. "That fool. Bested by a woman? Worthless."

"I never laid a hand on him."

Franklin's brow furrowed. "You mean he just gave me up?"

She laughed. "No, there was some persuading involved, but I wasn't the one doing it. My friend, Vasmir, helped with that." She let her smile fade. "He was only one of the gargoyles I was able to save."

Franklin's expression shifted again, this time to one of thinly veiled greed. "*You* saved one of the gargoyles. From the old hotel? But you showed me those pictures, you said they were all gone."

"I told you the only thing I could tell you. Because I didn't think anyone would believe the truth. Now I know better." She stuck the phone back into her pocket. "You know all about gargoyles, don't you, Franklin?"

He swallowed. "I-I've read a little about them, but..."

"You had my apartment ransacked because you saw the diamonds, knew I'd been going to the old hotel, knew who my grandfather was, and decided to see for yourself if the source of those diamonds was what you believed it to be."

For a moment, he did nothing. Then he lifted his chin defiantly. "My father is a very wealthy and powerful man. Name your price for the gargoyle. I know you need the money. Come on, what'll it be? Because one way or the other, I will own that beast."

He jabbed a finger at her. "Even if that means eliminating you. Better to take the money, don't you think?"

She hissed out a sigh through gritted teeth. "Gosh, that's such a great offer but I think Vasmir might have something to say about that himself." She grinned and raised her voice. "Vasmir, would you like to join us?"

# CHAPTER SEVENTEEN

Vasmir used two talons to separate the sliding glass doors until the gap was wide enough for him to enter. He stepped into the house, keeping his eyes on Franklin.

The human's eyes went wide as he took in Vasmir. A shiver shook the man-boy's narrow frame. The ice in his glass clinked.

Annaleigh held her hand out toward the man-boy. "Vasmir, this is Franklin. He wants to own you, even if that means eliminating me. Just wanted to bring you up to speed."

Anger seethed through Vasmir's body. He pinned Franklin with his gaze, inching closer to the man-boy, being careful with his footsteps, although he could feel his talons scraping the wood floors. He did not care. This was not a good person he was dealing with. "No one hurts Annaleigh. No one threatens Annaleigh."

Franklin gulped and held his hands up as best he could with his glass still in one of them. "I was just making a joke." He let out a thin laugh that sounded more like a sob and he crouched, setting his glass down. "I'd never hurt anyone."

"You sent a man to her apartment this evening."

"I did, you're right, and that was a terrible idea. I'm very sorry. I'll pay for whatever was broken or damaged and I promise I will never do anything like that ever again."

"No, you will not," Vasmir said. "And do you know why?"

Franklin sucked in a ragged breath. "Because you'll do something bad to me?"

Vasmir stared hard at Franklin. "What do you think is bad? Pain? Suffering? Having your limbs torn from your body?"

Franklin looked like he might cry. "I really don't want any trouble. I'm very sorry. I have some cash on me, Annaleigh can have all of that right now. I'll just go get my wallet and—"

"You will stay where you are."

Franklin nodded. "Right, yes. Not moving." He was shaking and seemed to be complying. Then he lunged for the coffee table and grabbed a decorative letter opener that had been laying atop some magazines. He swiped wildly at Vasmir.

Vasmir stepped closer, making no attempt to defend himself.

Franklin stabbed him with the letter opener. The blade snapped against Vasmir's skin, and clattered to the floor.

Vasmir took hold of Frankin's hand and squeezed until the handle fell to the floor as well. "I do not like you."

The blood drained from Franklin's face. He said nothing, just nodded.

Vasmir pulled Franklin closer until only a few inches remained between them. "I am going to show you what will happen to you if you bother Annaleigh or myself again."

"I don't think—"

Vasmir clamped hold of Franklin by his upper arms, gripping him carefully but firmly with his talons only skimming the skin.

Franklin shrieked then went limp. Vasmir held Franklin up and dragged him to the open sliding doors. Vasmir looked at Annaleigh. "I did not see him touch you, but I want to be sure. He did not hurt you, did he?"

"He didn't touch me. You're just going to teach him a lesson, right? You're not going to harm him?"

"A lesson, yes. One he will never forget. I won't be long."

She nodded, giving him a little smile. "I'll be here. Waiting."

Vasmir leaped into the sky, bringing Franklin along with him. He headed straight for the river as it was a location that seemed to make the biggest impression on humans. He shook Franklin slightly. "Wake up, human."

Franklin stirred, lifting his head. His eyes blinked

open and after a second, he seemed to grasp what was happening. He screamed.

Vasmir shook him again. "Stop that noise. No one can hear you. You are wasting your breath."

"My father is a very powerful man," Franklin repeated.

"Can he fly?" Vasmir asked.

Franklin stared at the water. His eyes rolled back in his head like he might pass out again.

Vasmir shook him to bring him back. "I know you know about my kind. What we are capable of. But such things are a gift to those who care for us. Not spoils to be taken by those who already have too much."

"I don't really have anything, it's all my father's..." Franklin glanced at him. "Please take me back. I promise I won't do anything to Annaleigh or you. I'll forget you exist, I swear it."

"I do not believe you. You say what you think you should. All while making plans to do something else." Vasmir flew higher. "You need to be shown what will happen if you attempt anything foolish."

"What are you going to do?" Franklin was trying to reach for Vasmir, to hold on to him, but Vasmir held him far enough away for that to be impossible.

He reached a good height and leveled off. "Remember this, human."

Then he released Franklin.

He screamed but it thinned out to a weak thread of sound as he fell.

Vasmir waited one more second, then dove. He caught Franklin by his right arm and leg just inches from the water. Vasmir skimmed the surface so that Franklin's dangling fingers touched liquid, then Vasmir ascended again.

Franklin wept. "I'm sorry," he whispered. "I'm so sorry."

Vasmir felt his point had been made, but Franklin was still a wretched example of humanity. "You should do something worthwhile with your money. Help those who have less than you do. Contribute to the world in some way. Make the world brighter. Not darker, like you do now."

Franklin nodded as best he could. "You're right, I should. I'm a terrible person. I'll do better."

Vasmir doubted he would. Most likely, Franklin would wake up tomorrow thinking his evening had just been a bad dream. That was fine with Vasmir, so long as Franklin left Annaleigh alone.

He spread his wings and glided to a stop in Franklin's small backyard. He released the human. Franklin lay on the patch of cropped grass and seemed to be trying to hug the earth.

Vasmir crouched next to him. "If you raise a finger against Annaleigh, all the evidence she has against you will go to the police. After that, I will come for you when you least expect it. I will snatch you off the street if I choose. You will not see me coming."

"You'll never hear from me again," Franklin muttered into the grass.

Vasmir straightened.

Annaleigh stepped out of the house. "How did it go?"

"He understands what he must do." Vasmir held his hand out to her. "Shall we go?"

She smiled at him. "I'm ready."

# CHAPTER EIGHTEEN

Annaleigh was nervous going into work the next day, but she couldn't leave all that money behind. It wouldn't be fair to Mr. Tidwell to just not show up either. She wanted to leave on good terms if possible so that she could get a reference from him.

She was also very curious to see if Franklin turned up or not. If he did, she was going to call Arnie's phone, which she'd left with Vasmir, and make him aware of the situation. What happened after that was all on Franklin.

Just like the day before, she'd arrived at the antique shop before anyone else. She hadn't slept much so getting in early hadn't been an issue. She was tired, but tonight would be different. Tonight, there'd be no mess to clean up, nothing to straighten, or put back together, or attempt to repair.

Maybe they'd have pizza again. Or she'd introduce Vasmir to the wonders of Chinese food. Anything that meant she didn't have to cook worked for her.

Their only real plan this evening was to look at available houses. They'd decided to head south, to slightly warmer weather not too far from the beach. Vasmir liked being near the water. She was happy to make him happy, and she had a great aunt living in Wrightsville Beach, North Carolina. Seemed like an easy decision to make.

She'd done a quick search of the homes for sale in the surrounding area, and there were some very nice places for reasonable amounts. It would mean selling a few more diamonds, but that should be simple enough.

The coffee was made by the time Mr. Tidwell arrived. "Annaleigh, you're in early again. Does that mean you decided to take the promotion I offered?"

She smiled. "As generous as that was, I've made a different decision, Mr. Tidwell. I'm moving to North Carolina to be near my great aunt." She shook her head. "I'm not cut out for city life. I've realized that."

Mr. Tidwell's face fell. "I'm sorry to hear we'll be losing you. I know I haven't been the best boss, and I apologize for that, but losing you and Franklin on the same day has me wondering if I was worse than I realized."

"You're losing Franklin?" Annaleigh blinked like that was news to her.

"Yes." Mr. Tidwell sighed. "He called last night to say he was taking some time off, effective immediately, to figure out what he wanted to do with his life. He had no idea when or if he'd be back." Mr. Tidwell rolled his eyes. "Fine with me. I only hired him as a favor to his father."

Annaleigh had nothing to lose. She decided to try a little truth. "You know his father is a shady character."

Mr. Tidwell snorted. "Do you really think I wanted to hire someone with no prior experience? I'm aware of who his father is. That's why Franklin got the job. You don't say no to Sebastian Fuller. Between us, I'm glad to see Franklin go. He was rubbish at his job anyway. Sucking up is no replacement for actual skill. Don't worry. I'll call the temp agency and have a replacement for him in no time."

Annaleigh laughed. "I should have given you more credit. And you weren't that bad of a boss."

"Moody, though. I know. My own fault. Business has been up and down quite a lot lately and I am too quick to snap at those around me. I must do better."

"I feel bad that you paid for my dinner last night, then."

"Don't. I'm writing it off as a business expense. But it was Franklin's idea to send you. He suggested it, anyway."

"Hmm." That didn't surprise her at all knowing what she knew now. "All the same, I'm sorry to hear business hasn't been the best."

"Don't be sorry. Those diamonds of yours have cemented some previously tenuous relationships with a couple of very wealthy customers. I've already had a referral for one of them. A woman on the upper east side who wants some showpieces for her new apartment. That sale alone might be worth half a million dollars."

"Great news."

"Indeed. I wish you had more of those stones."

"About that," Annaleigh said. "Maybe we should go into your office and have a discussion."

His brows lifted. "Are you saying you do have more?"

"I might have a few." She'd brought four with her. The blue and three larger, sparkling white ones.

His eyes narrowed suddenly. "Please tell me there's nothing dubious about these stones. Please. I don't think I could take any more bad news today."

"There's nothing dubious about them. They aren't stolen, they aren't blood diamonds, they aren't anything bad. My grandfather was just a wise and generous man who left me an incredible legacy." An image of Vasmir filled her head, making her smile.

Mr. Tidwell smiled back. "I would agree with you. Let's go have a look at what you brought."

She showed him the stones and they had a quick discussion about the possibility of selling a few more in the future. He promised to do right by her, and she believed him. She also promised to work for another week or two so that he could find a replacement for her.

The money for the pink diamond came in just before lunch and Mr. Tidwell gave her the check as promised. She used her break to deposit it at the bank.

Her account had never been so flush. When the other diamonds sold and she had that money, they'd be able to buy a house in cash.

She was excited to go home and start the search, even if it was such a big unknown. Moving felt a little daunting. Thankfully, she didn't have much to move.

That evening, she and Vasmir ate Chinese takeout and looked at all the homes available online. They found one that seemed perfect. A two thousand square foot rancher on three acres of land with lots of trees.

And it was one diamond less than she thought they'd have to pay.

"We should buy it," Vasmir said. "If you are happy with it."

"Don't you want to look at it?"

He squinted at the screen. "I am looking at it."

"I mean in person. We could drive down there this weekend. We have the money to rent a car. We could check out the area and—"

Vasmir put his arm around her and kissed her cheek. "We do not need a car. We can fly."

"All the way to North Carolina? Isn't that a long way for you to go? Won't you get tired?"

He laughed. "I did not mean I would fly. I meant we could take an airplane. I have always wanted to see what that was like."

"Oh. Right." She chuckled. "But you don't have any ID. You'd have to have one to get on a plane. To do most things these days, actually."

"How do I get an ID?"

"I don't really know. Sadly, Franklin probably would, but we do *not* need to be indebted to him."

"No, we do not."

"Tell you what. I'll ask Mr. Tidwell about it tomorrow. He's a pretty connected guy. He might know someone. And now that we have this diamond deal in place, I'm sure he'll help me."

"What are you going to tell him about me?"

"That you're a friend who's new to the city and needs some help. That's all true."

Vasmir nodded. "What if he thinks I am the source of the diamonds?"

"I don't think he will. I've basically told him the diamonds are an inheritance left by my grandfather. He seems to be happy with that explanation."

"Good. All right. See if he can help." He picked up the container of lo mein. "If not, we will rent the car."

"Then I'll email the realtor and see if we can look at the house on Saturday." Happiness filled her as she typed out a quick message, making sure to mention it would be a cash deal.

Unsurprisingly, the realtor responded almost instantly.

# EPILOGUE

One Year Later

Vasmir touched down at the very back of the property, shielded by the trees that surrounded their land. He shook out his wings, then shifted into his human form and walked toward the house. The roses that Annaleigh had planted by the deck perfumed the warm air and stars were beginning to appear overhead. It was a beautiful night. Perfect for flying.

Better for being at home.

Annaleigh was in the garden. She had a basket on her arm. It was filled with the last of the summer's tomatoes. She walked toward him, smiling, the fat diamond on her ring finger flashing in the lights from the house. "How was your flight?"

"It was very good."

"I wasn't sure, you came back early."

He took the basket from her and put it on the ground. Then he pulled her into his arms and pressed his lips to her temple. "I missed my wife." She smelled of lemons and soap. Everything about her made him happy.

She leaned into him. "I miss flying with you."

He touched the soft curve of her belly. It seemed to grow every day. "It won't be long before you will again. Both of you."

She looked up at him. "That will be something, won't it?"

He nodded. Thinking about his child made him emotional. Thinking about his new life did the same. He'd come so close to being destroyed, now... He sniffed, trying to hold back the feelings welling up inside him.

"It makes me weepy, too. All this happiness." Annaleigh sniffed, just like he had, and patted his chest. "I never thought we'd have a life like this. I never thought I would anyway. A house of my own with an amazing husband and a little one on the way...it's just so much more than I ever dreamed of."

Her words were all it took. He nodded as a single fat tear rolled down his cheek. "I feel the same."

Annaleigh looked up in time to catch the diamond before it fell to the grass. She held it up between her fingers so that the light from the house illuminated it. "That might be one of the biggest ones yet. I guess we can safely say junior's college fund is taken care of."

"Can a gargoyle go to college?"

She blinked. "Is this baby going to be a gargoyle?"

"I guess we will know if he comes out with wings."

Her eyes widened.

"I am teasing you. He or she will be half of me and half of you and completely perfect." He smiled and picked her up in his arms.

She let out a little squeal and laughed. "Where are we going?"

"Inside," Vasmir said. "Flying has given me an appetite."

"We already ate dinner."

He nuzzled his face against her throat, inhaling her tantalizing aroma and savoring the warmth of her skin. "Food is not what I am hungry for."

With a soft giggle, she wrapped her arms around his neck. "Oh, I see." She sighed. "You know, your year is up tomorrow."

He stopped just inside the back door and looked at her. "Is it? I did not realize."

She nodded. "After tomorrow, you're no longer bound to me by the rules of your kind."

He used his foot to close the door. "I will always be bound to you, Annaleigh. You are she who called me. And now I am he who loves you."

She clasped his face in her hands, her eyes shining with pleasure. "I love you, too."

"And you are happy?"

"I am happier than I have words to express."

"Good. I want to always make you happy." He smiled as he carried her toward the bedroom. "But perhaps I can improve on that even more."

PARANORMAL WOMEN'S FICTION

**Midlife Fairy Tale Series:**

The Accidental Queen

The Summer Palace

**First Fangs Club Series:**

Sucks To Be Me

Suck It Up Buttercup

Sucker Punch

The Suck Stops Here

Embrace The Suck

**Code Name: Mockingbird** (A Paranormal Women's Fiction Novella)

COZY MYSTERY:

**Jayne Frost Series:**

Miss Frost Solves A Cold Case: A Nocturne Falls Mystery

Miss Frost Ices The Imp: A Nocturne Falls Mystery

Miss Frost Saves The Sandman: A Nocturne Falls Mystery

Miss Frost Cracks A Caper: A Nocturne Falls Mystery

When Birdie Babysat Spider: A Jayne Frost Short

Miss Frost Braves The Blizzard: A Nocturne Falls Mystery

Miss Frost Chills The Cheater: A Nocturne Falls Mystery

Miss Frost Says I Do: A Nocturne Falls Mystery

Lost in Las Vegas: A Frost And Crowe Mystery

Wrapped up in Christmas: A Frost And Crowe Mystery

Mystified In Music City: A Frost And Crowe Mystery

**HappilyEverlasting Series:**

Witchful Thinking

PARANORMAL ROMANCE

**Nocturne Falls Series:**

The Vampire's Mail Order Bride

The Werewolf Meets His Match

The Gargoyle Gets His Girl

The Professor Woos The Witch

The Witch's Halloween Hero – short story

The Werewolf's Christmas Wish – short story

The Vampire's Fake Fiancée

The Vampire's Valentine Surprise – short story

The Shifter Romances The Writer

The Vampire's True Love Trials – short story

The Dragon Finds Forever

The Vampire's Accidental Wife

The Reaper Rescues The Genie

The Detective Wins The Witch

The Vampire's Priceless Treasure

The Werewolf Dates The Deputy

The Siren Saves The Billionaire

The Vampire's Sunny Sweetheart

Death Dates The Oracle

**Shadowvale Series:**

The Trouble With Witches

The Vampire's Cursed Kiss

The Forgettable Miss French

Moody And The Beast

Her First Taste Of Fire

Monster In The Mirror

A Sky Full Of Stars

**Sin City Collectors Series**

Queen Of Hearts

Dead Man's Hand

Double or Nothing

**Standalone Paranormal Romance:**

Dark Kiss of the Reaper

Heart of Fire

Recipe for Magic

Miss Bramble and the Leviathan

All Fired Up

URBAN FANTASY

**The House of Comarré series:**

Forbidden Blood

Blood Rights

Flesh and Blood

Bad Blood

Out For Blood

Last Blood

**The Crescent City series:**

House of the Rising Sun

City of Eternal Night

Garden of Dreams and Desires

*Want to be up to date on all books & release dates by Kristen Painter? Sign-up for my newsletter on my website, www.kristenpainter.com. No spam, just news (sales, freebies, and releases.)*

*If you loved the book and want to help the series grow, tell a friend about the book and take time to leave a review!*

*Nothing is completed without an amazing team.*

*Many thanks to:*

*Cover design: Cover design and composite cover art by Janet Holmes using images from Shutterstock.com & Depositphotos.com.*
*Interior formatting: Gem Promotions*
*Editor/Copyedits: Chris Kridler*
*Proofs: Nancy Brunori*

Made in the USA
Middletown, DE
21 February 2026